ON TOP OF THE WORLD

THE TORONTO STAR'S TRIBUTE TO THE '92 BLUE JAYS

Remember that wonderful scene where the Wizard of Oz gives the cowardly lion a medal to prove he has courage.

The Blue Jays have just done that for Toronto. We've known for years that we were a big league city. Now we've got the proof to show the world.

Right from the start, this was a team that gave us a reason to hope and cheer, especially in times when Toronto and the whole country desperately needed something to get excited about.

The Star has been there for every game played by the Jays since they debuted in the snow of Exhibition Stadium on April 7, 1977. We suffered with them when they lost nearly twice as many games as they won. We celebrated with them when they won three other American League East championships. But nothing has come close to the sheer joy of their '92 triumph.

We thank them for that and are pleased to be able to salute them with this book filled with wonderful memories from an historic year.

John Honderich

John Honderich, Editor
The Toronto Star

TEXT:
GEORGE GAMESTER and GERRY HALL
with contributions from Neil MacCarl, Dave Perkins and The Toronto Star sports staff

EDITORS:
BRAD HENDERSON and GERRY HALL

PHOTO EDITOR:
BRAD HENDERSON

ART DIRECTOR:
IAN SOMERVILLE
with contributions from Susan McDonough and Kathleen Doody

COPY EDITOR:
ROB GRANT

PRODUCTION:
WILLIAM ARBON
with contributions from Bruce Wilson and Mario Ardizzi

TECHNICIANS:
ALAN MCARTHUR, DOMENIC BATTAGLIA, AL WYATT, STEVE WOODS, DAVE BURGESS AND KEVIN OMURA

ILLUSTRATIONS:
PATRICK CORRIGAN

PHOTOGRAPHY:
TORONTO STAR STAFF PHOTOGRAPHERS

COVER PHOTO BY MICHAEL SLAUGHTER

Color by Superior Graphics
Produced by The Toronto Star for:

Publisher:
Doubleday Canada Limited
Copyright 1992, Toronto Star
Newspapers Limited

Printed and bound in Canada
(Reprinted 1992)

PLAY IT AGAIN

You never knew whether it would be heartburn or heaven when the '92 Blue Jays took the field.

Sometimes they won ugly, and sometimes they lost ugly. But mostly they won beautiful, so beautiful you could almost taste it.

Finally, they went into the heart of Dixie and won it all. Canada's first World Series, the championship of the universe — unless there's a team on Mars we don't know about. Play it again, Joe and Robbie, Dave and Jimmy, Pat and Devo, Juan and everyone. We'll never get tired of listening.

The World Series. The best bit of cross-border shopping ever. The greatest moment in Toronto sports history — and right now, we don't care if hearing that makes Conn Smythe twirl in his grave like a Tasmanian devil.

The Jays did it with a hired gun and a fallen hero. They did it with the friskiest 41-year-old on the planet, and with a guy who gives a money-back guarantee on 100 RBIs a season. They did it with the classiest lefty who ever came out of Alabama without a banjo, and with kids who pitched, hit and fielded their way out of the barrios of Latin America. They also did it with an unknown minor leaguer who deposited the first World Series pitch he ever saw over the fence for a two-run, game-winning homer.

They never did it the easy way, as surviving couch potatoes from the championship game can attest. But maybe there is no easy way to be the best baseball team in the world. As Sherpa guide Tenzing Norgay used to say, "There's no elevator service to the top of Mount Everest."

They did it with the most second-guessed manager in baseball. In the eyes of his critics, Cito Gaston could do nothing right — except win.

They did it mostly in an extravagant, $600 million palace built for grown men to play little boys' games.

They did it in a prosperous but recession-plagued city in which some people still live in the streets and others depend on food banks to help them feed their families. But when a panhandler hits you up for a loonie on the way home from a game and asks you how the Jays did, you realize just how much he and you need the promise of better things to come that this team delivered.

Just ask the 45,551 fans who yelled themselves hoarse watching the final game from Atlanta on the world's biggest TV screen at the SkyDome, or the 500,000 who partied on Yonge St. afterwards, how much this team has meant to them.

It wasn't even a case of our Americans beating their Americans. Like the city itself, the Jays featured a cosmopolitan cast. Key players hailed from Puerto Rico, the Dominican Republic and Jamaica, as well as every part of the U.S. except the home of the Yankees. For part of the season, there was even that rarest of all birds, a role player born in Toronto.

They've left us with so much to remember and so little to forget. Close your eyes and watch Devon White one more

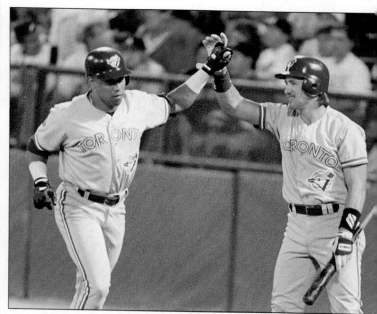

COLIN McCONNELL

WORLD SERIES HOMER BY CANDY MALDONADO GETS HIM A HIGH FIVE FROM ON-DECK BATTER PAT BORDERS.

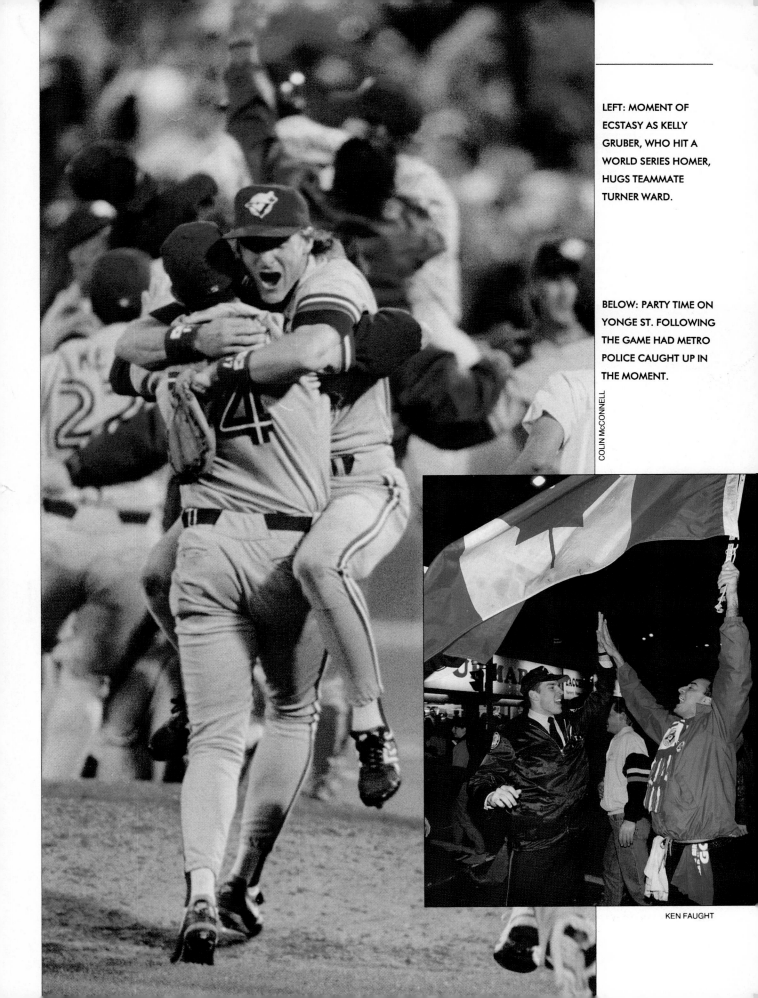

LEFT: MOMENT OF ECSTASY AS KELLY GRUBER, WHO HIT A WORLD SERIES HOMER, HUGS TEAMMATE TURNER WARD.

BELOW: PARTY TIME ON YONGE ST. FOLLOWING THE GAME HAD METRO POLICE CAUGHT UP IN THE MOMENT.

COLIN McCONNELL

KEN FAUGHT

time, gliding across the outfield and making an improbable catch look like your granny could have done it. You knew he would save his best grab of all for when it really mattered. The Catch, as grandchildren in the 21st century will be told again and again, was the difference in Game 3 of the Series.

Watch again as Robbie Alomar bellyflops to his right on a hard smash and throws a batter out from his knees for the zillionth time — okay, so maybe it was only 15, but one of them came in the final game of the World Series. Somehow it seems fitting that the best of all Jays scored both the first and last runs of their greatest season.

Hear that crack of the bat? It's Joe Carter or Dave Winfield cashing in another runner, 227 between them during the sea-

COLIN McCONNELL

TOO LATE TO DOUBLE UP BRAVES SHORTSTOP JEFF BLAUSER,
ROBBIE ALOMAR LEAPS OVER HIM IN SERIES ACTION.

son. You won't be alone in remembering the last crack of all, Winfield's smash down the third base line that scored White and Alomar. Winfield says it was the greatest moment of his 2,730-game career.

Sure, Jack Morris failed miserably as Mr. October, which is what the Jays thought they were buying for their $5 million. But what an April through September he gave them, becoming the first 20-game winner in team history. He's the guy who showed fans, right from the get-go, that this was a different team.

Remember how he refused to be yanked in the ninth inning on opening day in Detroit, even though he was nearing 145 pitches? Remember him hurling nine scoreless innings in June to outduel Rocket Roger Clemens?

Some of the most beautiful memories from the season bloomed in the dog days of summer, after the team went into a tailspin and the relentless Orioles closed to within half a game.

The Jays picked a three-game series with the world champion Minnesota Twins to end the bleeding, sweeping them at the SkyDome. A guy named Ed Sprague, recently recalled from the minors, supplied all the runs needed in the final come-from-behind win with a three-run homer. If he never did another thing all season, he'd earned his pay there. Who would have dreamed he would repeat his heroics to win Game 2 of the Series?

That sweep of the Twins, you may recall, came after Winfield had urged subdued Toronto fans to grab a mitt and get into the game. "The fans need us and we need them," he said. "We feed off each other."

Anyway, the pep talk and sweep helped us forget the Friday night massacre of Aug. 28, when the Brewers smacked an American League record 31 hits off six Jays pitchers and beat Toronto 22-2. It also allowed us to be more forgiving of David Cone's disastrous AL debut against the fast-closing Brew Crew. The Jays' hired gun gave up seven runs and seven stolen bases to Phil Garner's flying circus before righting himself and winning four key games with a 2.55 ERA.

Remember Jimmy Key, suffering through his worst season but coming alive to win his last five games? That got the brass wondering if he might not be useful in post-season play, after all. Remember Juan Guzman, clinching the divisional title on the second-last day and the playoffs, just when it looked as if Oakland might come back?

The rest is much fresher in our minds: Alomar's crucial two-run homer to tie Game 4 of the AL playoffs, in which the Jays had been down 6-1; Derek Bell, scoring the winning run on Pat Borders' clutch 11th-inning sacrifice fly.

Memories of the Series are still crowding each other out. Borders' MVP performance at the plate and the dramatic end he and David Wells put to all those steals; Candy Maldonado and Kelly Gruber belting key homers; Duane Ward and Key winning all four games between them, while the big-money imports were shut out; Jane Fonda, praying for a win, or maybe for the Tomahawk Chop to stop.

What follows is a detailed look at the Blue Jays' greatest season, from the Christmas shopping that brought in Morris and Winfield to the heroics of an unknown rookie and the return of Key as the Jay you could count on when the chips were down.

PARADE OF CHAMPIONS.
TENS OF THOUSANDS
OF FANS LINE THE WAY
AS THE JAYS AND THEIR
FAMILIES DRIVE TO
SKYDOME ON THE
MONDAY FOLLOWING
THE FINAL GAME FOR
THE BIGGEST LOVE-IN IN
TORONTO'S HISTORY.
"WE'RE ALL NUMBER
ONE," JOE CARTER TELLS
FANS WHO JAM THE
DOME FOR A FINAL
TRIBUTE TO THE WORLD
SERIES WINNERS.

BERNARD WEIL

BIG DEAL

There were only seven days left till Christmas, and Paul Beeston still had two big items left on his shopping list: an American League championship and a World Series.

The Blue Jays president knew in his heart that frigid December day that the people he was buying for wouldn't be satisfied with anything less than the former, and he knew they would love him forever if he lucked into the latter.

It was becoming clear to Beeston, however, that the price was so high that it would have made George Steinbrenner blanch in the days when he was trying to put together the best team money could buy.

The specific item Beeston was looking at was a 36-year-old pitcher with more than 3,000 innings on his muscular right arm. Jack Morris had come to the bigs to stay in 1977, the same year the Blue Jays were born. Not only would he be the oldest Jay, but the highest paid, too. It would take $5 million a year to land Morris; he wanted $1.85 million for his signature alone. What a time for general manager Pat Gillick to be away on a Caribbean holiday.

Beeston was aware that pitching deals usually turned out to be poison for the Jays. His stomach muscles still tightened when visions of Bill Caudill, Ken Dayley and Tom Candiotti danced in his head.

Still, Beeston reasoned, Jack Morris was different. He knew how to win. More important, he knew how to win the big ones. Just last year, Morris was the key factor in taking the Minnesota Twins, who had finished last in 1990, to a World Series championship.

Beeston must have drooled in anticipation of his meeting with Morris and his agent, Dick Moss, as he re-ran mind movies of Game 7 of the '91 Series: the one in which Morris, making his 40th start of the season, trudged back to the mound time after time in a 10-inning, 1-0 win. Earlier, Morris had been the difference in the playoffs, beating the Jays twice.

As Beeston prepared for his 9 a.m. meeting in the Jays' SkyDome offices on Dec. 18, he knew his club wasn't the only one in the running. In fact, Moss and Morris had airline tickets to Boston in their pockets.

Eight hours later, they had cancelled their flight and the Jays had made the second-biggest deal in their 15-year history, topped only by the 1990 blockbuster that brought in Joe Carter and Roberto Alomar in exchange for Fred McGriff and four-time Gold Glover Tony Fernandez.

In Morris, the Jays had landed the winningest pitcher in

JEFF GOODE

BLUE JAYS PRESIDENT PAUL BEESTON MADE WORLD SERIES
GAMBLE IN HIS OFFICE AT SKYDOME WHEN HE SIGNED JACK
MORRIS FOR $5 MILLION A YEAR.

TONY BOCK

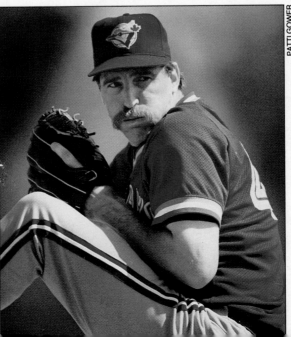

PATTI GOWER

FIERY COMPETITOR
MORRIS WON HIS SERIES
OPENER IN DETROIT
(ABOVE) AND SHOWED
HE WAS A TEAM PLAYER
IN SPRING BY WORKING
HARDER THAN MOST
ROOKIES. HE BECAME
FIRST 20-GAME WINNER
IN CLUB HISTORY.

RICK EGLINTON

THE DAY AFTER SIGNING MORRIS, JAYS GAVE $2.3 MILLION FOR DAVE WINFIELD, THE FRISKIEST 40-YEAR-OLD ON THE FACE OF THE PLANET, AS HE SHOWS HERE IN AUGUST ACTION AGAINST ONE OF HIS FORMER TEAMS, THE YANKEES.

COLIN McCONNELL

their history, 216-162 in the regular season, 7-1 in post-season play; a hurler who was a good bet to pitch himself into Cooperstown. Still, there seemed little reason to believe he would become the first 20-game winner in Jays history; he hadn't won 20 since '86.

Moreover, no one knew then that his presence would be necessary just to finish first in the American League East — never mind the playoffs. Few suspected those other birds, so dismal in '91 in Baltimore, would be on the Blue Jays' tail nearly all season long and that Morris would be the only starter that skipper Cito Gaston could count on in August.

The Jays realized they were getting a tough and fiery competitor, on and off the field. The way he treated female reporters who ventured into the locker room after a game made Victor Kiam look like Sir Walter Raleigh.

Tigers manager Sparky Anderson, who could find something nice to say about Dracula, said Morris could be "the nastiest, most self-centred man" he had ever met. Minnesota fans said even worse things when they found out he was deserting their beloved Twins after one glorious year in the town where he was born (St. Paul).

Morris had broken down and cried after pitching the Twins into the Series, and fans couldn't be blamed for feeling he would play out his days there.

One factor — besides money — that helped the recently divorced Morris make up his mind was the fact that his two sons were going to school in not-too-distant Detroit. Morris, however, credited "the smooth talk of Paul Beeston. He's a real charmer."

Later, Morris told the press, "I believe in this team. I believe it can win and, if you don't know me, I like winning."

Beeston seemed equally impressed with Morris.

"You wouldn't mind being with him in a bunker in the war," he said after signing the contract that would give Morris $15 million over three years.

Morris wasn't the club's oldest player for long, though. Within 24 hours, the Jays had also signed legendary slugger Dave Winfield, who would be making perhaps his final stop on the way to the Hall of Fame.

Winfield — 40, frisky and a free agent — was signed to a one-year deal for $2.3 million, probably the best bargain in team history. The braintrust had gone to the Miami winter meetings early in December, looking primarily for a starting pitcher and a designated hitter. They had come home from the '90 meetings in Chicago with Alomar, Carter and Devon White, but this time they struck out. They didn't start hitting for the downs till they got back to frigid Toronto.

It was clear that something had to be done about the DH spot when the sundry players who filled in there in '91 finished last in the AL in homers and RBIs (five and 56). Moreover, although great things were expected of young John Olerud, it was far from clear that he was ready to give the kind of protection a No. 4 hitter should give to Carter, the team's leading run producer.

Playing for the anemic California Angels, where he was often the only dangerous hitter in sight, the classy Winfield had still managed to hit 28 homers and drive in 86 runs.

From the moment he'd signed, however, Winfield had made it clear he didn't consider himself a one-dimensional player; his outfielder's glove wasn't quite ready for a glass case in Cooperstown.

"When they see physically what I am able to do, they're going to see there's a lot of versatility left in me," he told Star baseball writer Allan Ryan. "Toronto got a real bargain here. They're going to be very happy with me; I'm going to be very

JEFF GOODE

SEEMED LIKE A MINOR MOVE WHEN JAYS RE-SIGNED AGING ALFREDO GRIFFIN BUT HE PLAYED IMPORTANT LATE-SEASON ROLE.

happy with them."

Winfield had always been popular in Toronto, even after he accidentally killed a seagull with a thrown ball at the Ex in '83 and was charged by police: "First time he hit the cutoff man all year," the late Billy Martin quipped.

His popularity with Jays fans would soar to within sight of Alomar's cloud nine. Winfield quickly established himself as the greatest DH in club history, upping his average by more than 30 points and becoming the first player over 40 to ever drive in more than 100 runs. For Winfield, it would be the eighth time he had surpassed the century mark.

All of a sudden, Carter was seeing strikes from pitchers who would have walked him in '91, rather than giving him anything good to hit. As a result, Carter scored even more runs and drove in more than he had in '91.

PETER POWER

Moreover, Olerud slowly began to show signs of the greatness that had been predicted for him since he joined the team without having played a game in the minors.

Before the winter was over, the Jays had made a small move that would pay dividends when a mysterious knee ailment put shortstop Manuel Lee on the shelf. Alfredo Griffin, the once starry Jays shortstop who had been sent west thanks to the fielding magic of Tony Fernandez, was signed to a minor league contract.

As the Jays headed for spring training, you couldn't blame the brass for feeling the team would win the pennant — even without a reincarnated Dave Stieb, or a Kelly Gruber who could play third base and hit like the Gruber of '90.

With 34 games to go, though, and the pitching still too iffy for comfort, they went back to the Labatt piggy bank one more time and nabbed the National League's strikeout king, David Cone. Generally regarded as one of the top dozen pitchers in baseball, the 29-year-old New York Met was to become a free agent at the end of the year. The Mets were already paying him $4.25 million and were unlikely to keep him at the stratospheric pricetag he would command.

The Jays weren't worried about that. If Cone could help them win the World Series, he could go wherever he wanted in '93. So, they sent infielder Jeff Kent, a promising 24-year-old with pop in his bat, and minor league outfielder Ryan Thompson to the Mets for Cone — who was happy enough to get out of New York (where he'd had personal problems), especially to a winning team.

Kent had become a fan favorite while filling in for Gruber at third, but was considered expendable because he couldn't do much to deliver a pennant in '92, especially from the bench.

One thing that became evident after the deal was that the Jays, with their record-smashing crowds, could no longer be considered underdogs or poor cousins. They were definitely among the fat cats of the majors with a payroll around $43 million, just below what the Mets and Dodgers were paying for mediocrity. The Jays, however, had reason to expect that their money had bought much, much more.

COLIN McCONNELL

JEFF KENT (LEFT) OPENED EYES DURING SPRING TRAINING AND BECAME AN EARLY-SEASON FAN FAVORITE FILLING IN FOR OFT-INJURED KELLY GRUBER. MARK EICHHORN (RIGHT) WAS RE-ACQUIRED IN A TRADE THAT SENT CANADIAN OUTFIELDER ROB DUCEY AND CATCHER GREG MYERS TO CALIFORNIA.

RICHARD LAUTENS

WITH ONLY 34 GAMES TO GO, THE JAYS ACQUIRED MAJOR LEAGUE STRIKEOUT KING DAVID CONE IN THE TRADE THAT SENT KENT TO NEW YORK. IT WASN'T HARD TO SPOT THE PITCHER'S FAN CLUB AT SKYDOME AS CONE HEADS MADE AN IMMEDIATE APPEARANCE.

RICHARD LAUTENS

HIGH HOPES

In spring, when a young man's fancy lightly turns to thoughts of hot dogs, beer and rockets to right field, even the Seattle Mariners find reasons for hope. But, reporting for spring training at the Cecil P. Englebert Complex in Dunedin, Fla., last March, the Toronto Blue Jays had more than hope on their side. They had Jack Morris and Dave Winfield.

Two of baseball's greatest stars had been added to the roster over the winter at a cost of more than $7 million for the year — nine times what the Jays paid their whole team when they broke into the league in 1977.

Without these two worthies, the Jays had cleaned up in the weak-sister American League East Division in 1991 but fizzled in the playoffs. With them, a solid shot at its first World Series crown appeared within Toronto's grasp.

Moreover, fans with faces scrunched against the security gates at Englebert Field for their first glimpse at the former Jay killers in a friendly uniform, realized as well as the club's brass did that this was a now-or-never season. Blow it and stars like Joe Carter and Jimmy Key likely would be lost to the big bucks of free agency at season's end. That would leave the Jays to do battle using a formula they had abandoned more than a year ago — trying to win with players developed through their farm system.

Now, the team that took the field for the muscle-wrenching conditioning exercises devised by fitness expert Rick Knox was dominated by stars who had been bought rather than developed — Joe Carter, Robbie Alomar and Devon White in major 1990 trades, and Morris and Winfield in last winter's free agency market.

But few really cared. Toronto needed something to root for. It and the rest of the country were caught in the worst recession since the '30s, unemployment was at a seven-year high and the hockey Leafs were once more bound for oblivion, even without Harold Ballard's help.

So, bring on the New Jays! This March, we really needed their promise of good things to come, a spring tonic for what ailed us.

Happily, this promised to be the easiest spring training in the club's history. George Bell was now a distant memory and the riddles to be solved in the Florida sunshine

HEY, WHO'S GOING TO SIGN MY BALL? A YOUNG FAN AT DUNEDIN FINDS OUT THAT YOU HAVE TO WORK AT ATTRACTING PLAYERS EVEN IN THE CLOSE CONFINES OF SPRING TRAINING.

PATTI GOWER

PATTI GOWER

MOMENT OF TRUTH. JACK MORRIS AND DAVE STIEB SHARE A CUBICLE FOR AN EYE EXAMINATION DURING MEDICALS AT DUNEDIN. SECONDS LATER, THE FORMER ENEMIES STARED HARD AT EACH OTHER, THEN BEGAN TO CHUCKLE.

LEAPING LIZARDS? NO, JUST JOE CARTER JUMPING OVER MANUEL LEE TO LIGHTEN UP A TRAINING SESSION.

were simple enough for even the manager of the Bad News Bears to handle. The only major questions left unanswered were these:

☐ Who would be in left field?

☐ Who would be the fifth starter?

☐ Who would be at short?

As long as the answer to any of those questions wasn't Dick Stuart, the Jays were going to do okay. There wasn't a manager in baseball who wouldn't trade his last plug of tobacco to have so little to worry about.

Mind you, there were a few nagging little questions. For starters: Which Kelly Gruber would show up to play third? And would Pat Borders ever learn to block the plate against errant pitches and bulldozing runners? And, please, would John Olerud become less willing to take a walk this year and leadoff hitter Devon White be-

PATTI GOWER

HOW DID BATTING PRACTICE GO ON THIS SUNNY DAY IN MARCH? YOU GUESS.

come a little more willing to do so?

Minor stuff really. Nothing that should take a whole month in Florida to figure out. But it's so much fun to see grown men cry as they shed the residue of last winter's banquet-circuit second helpings that the Jays decide to go ahead with spring training after all.

Right from the start, there are some neat little scenes at Dunedin as the grumbling over pushups, leg crunches and forearm stretches begins. There's trimmed-down, new papa David Wells holding forth on the proper way to burp a baby. And Cito Gaston lifting his shirt to show off the ugly scar from the back operation that relieved the terrible pain which had driven him from the dugout during the second half of the '91 season.

Then there's that delicious moment of truth when bitter, old enemies Morris and Dave Stieb find themselves sharing the same cubicle for an eye examination. They stare hard at each other, then chuckle. But does Stieb forget the day when Morris called him a quitter for taking himself out of a game in the sixth inning? Does Morris forget Stieb's crusty reply that he didn't want to be like Morris, staying for nine innings no matter how many runs he gave up? Everyone knows the answer to those questions, but at least the hatchet is sheathed, if not buried.

Morris, who checked in toting a Minnesota Twins duffel bag, was 22 minutes late for this first day as a Jay. But it wasn't by design. "It took me an hour to find this place," he said. "Somebody gave me bad directions."

He arrived, however, saying the kind of things the Jays had been wanting to hear from their pitchers since the team was hatched in snowy Exhibition Stadium in 1977.

"You're only as good as your last game," he told reporters who pressed in around him after his first day. "Fortunately, my last game was a good one (the 10-inning, 1-0, seventh-game shutout that won the Series for the Twins).

"I got to spend the whole winter with that feeling. But when I pitch my first game here this spring, that will all be in the past. And I have to look at it that way.

"The past doesn't mean a heck of a lot. It is a team sport. Everybody has to do his part. My approach has never really changed. I give it all I've got. When I go to bed at night, if I know I've given 100 per cent, I can sleep."

Another late arrival was shortstop Manuel Lee. But he was two days late, despite the fact he was regarded as one of the question marks for the Jays as they prepared for their greatest season.

Though he had played well in the field in his first full year at shortstop, Lee had batted only .234 in '91 and had looked like a feeble old lady swatting flies during many of his 107 strikeouts. Once again there was talk of him losing his job to slick-fielding Eddie Zosky, who arrived in camp 10 days before Lee and was working hard to convince the brass he could be a top shortstop in the majors as he had been with Syracuse of the International League in '91.

But Lee didn't seem too worried. "I got experience; nothing bothers me," he told Star baseball reporter Allan Ryan. As it turned out, Lee was right not to worry. Zosky had a terrible spring, batting 12 points lighter than his 175-pound weight and being dispatched back to Syracuse before the team headed north.

Zosky, who reacted angrily when the same thing happened after the '91 camp, behaved much more like a professional this time. "I'm going to go down there and force them to bring me back up," he said as he packed his bags for Triple-A.

But a much less heralded rookie infielder, Jeff Kent, opened some eyes with his Florida hitting (.375 in 28 games with a home run and six RBIs). The 24-year-old Kent had a problem, however; he was a second baseman and that posi-

14

PATTI GOWER

RBIs WERE SLOW IN COMING TO JOHN OLERUD THIS SPRING BUT THE COACHING STAFF, WATCHING HIS FLAWLESS SWING, WERE STILL CERTAIN HE WOULD BE A FUTURE MAJOR LEAGUE STAR.

MANNY LEE SHOWS OFF THE NUMBER OF HIS DOMINICAN ISLAND BUDDY ALFREDO GRIFFIN, WHO CHECKED INTO CAMP AFTER BEING SIGNED TO A MINOR LEAGUE CONTRACT. LATER, GRIFFIN FILLED IN WELL FOR THE INJURED LEE AT SHORTSTOP.

PATTI GOWER

tion was expected to be occupied with the Jays for, say, the next decade or so.

"I had a blast," said Kent as he and Zosky headed back to Syracuse. It wasn't his last blast as things turned out. He was recalled early in April and made a major contribution, mostly subbing at third for the oft-injured Kelly Gruber.

In 65 games, Kent became a fan favorite in Toronto as his key hits drove in 35 runs. Many were sorry to see him depart late in August as part of the deal with the Mets for strikeout king David Cone.

As far as left field was concerned, most observers had already accorded it to Derek Bell before a single Grapefruit League contest had taken place. The happy-go-lucky Floridian had been chosen by *Baseball America* as '91 minor league player of the year after batting .346 at Syracuse, with 93 RBIs and 27 stolen bases. Goodbye Candy Maldonado was what the March winds were sighing, especially after Bell took off at a torrid pace in the sunshine of his home state.

There was talk that Maldonado had lost some of the bat speed that made him a pleasant surprise in left field when he was acquired late last season for about what a Big Mac and a Coke cost at SkyDome.

He had hit .250 with 12 homers and 48 RBIs in 288 at-bats and played much better left field than George Bell ever did. But no one seemed to remember any more that this 30-year-old Puerto Rican had driven in 95 runs for the Cleveland Indians in 1990.

He had tested the free agent market after that sparkling season, asking for $2 million and being offered nothing. Finally he landed with Milwaukee, but went down with a broken bone in his foot after getting his first hit for the Brewers. That's how the Jays got him so cheaply last year. Now he was being written off — a trifle prematurely as things turned out — as Bell snatched left field from under him.

NOT A FASHION PLATE BUT A NEW FATHER, RELIEVER DAVID WELLS, HELD FORTH AT CAMP ON THE BEST WAY TO BURP A BABY.

WINFIELD SHOWS HE COMES TO PLAY EVEN IN SPRING, SLIDING TO BEAT A THROW TO THE PLATE IN A GAME AGAINST THE ROYALS.

MICHAEL STUPARYK

So all that was left for Gaston was to find that fifth starter to go along with a front four that was the stingiest in baseball. In 1991, the Jays staff had posted a 3.50 ERA, with Juan Guzman going 10-3 with a 2.99 ERA; Jimmy Key, 16-12 (3.05); Todd Stottlemyre, 15-8 (3.78); and David (Boomer) Wells, 15-10 (3.72).

Now the Jays had Morris, with his 18-12 (3.43) record, so they had their man, right? Not exactly. There was still a suspicion that Wells was better as a reliever and was more valuable as a lefthanded setup man for closers Duane Ward and Tom Henke.

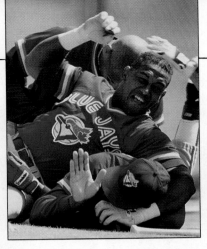

What about Dave Stieb, the erstwhile, almost perfect ace of the staff, its winningest pitcher and author of the team's only no-hitter? Last year had been a disaster for him, although at 4-3, he posted his 10th winning season in 13 big league years. A herniated disk had ended Stieb's '91 season in May and he faced a long battle back from a Dec. 4 operation to correct it.

His spring appearance at Dunedin convinced the club's brass and its fans that Stieb had a way to go in his comeback. And many who saw him were left wondering if he would be much help in '92. Unfortunately, when he did get back into the lineup, their worst fears were realized.

One thing was certain: The Jays would look a lot more closely at the young pitchers they had in camp than they did in 1991 when they gave Guzman only a cursory glance, although he had pitched as well as anyone and better than most.

MIDDLE: YOUNG FAN IMPROVISES TO COAX AN AUTOGRAPH FROM HIS JAY HERO.

BOTTOM: NEEDLE TIME CAN'T BE THAT BAD, CAN IT, JOE?

PATTI GOWER

At the time he was a 24-year-old non-roster pitcher from the Dominican Republic, whom the Jays had obtained from the Dodgers in a deal that sent second baseman Mike Sharperson west. In 1990, Guzman was third in the league in strikeouts at Double-A Knoxville, and 7-1 in the Dominican in winter ball. The book on him read: a righthander with a blazing fastball and control problems.

Guzman was an early '91 cut despite the fact his two Florida performances were as good as the Jays got. One was a six-inning start in a B-squad game against the Phillies that the Jays won 3-1. Nonetheless, he was shipped off to Syracuse. He didn't attract much attention until June, when an emergency replacement was needed and it was noted he had struck out 67 Triple-A batters in as many innings.

Down the stretch in '91, Guzman was the ace of the staff, winning a club record 10 in a row. He was also the only Jay to buy a win in the playoffs. The fact he never got to pitch a second game in the championship series was still sticking in the craw of many fans and was one of the biggest sources of criticism about Gaston's post-season managing.

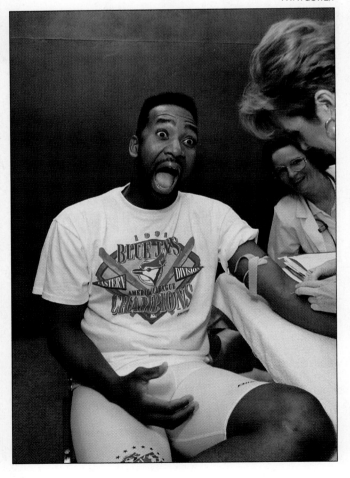

The '91 Jays had also gone south seeking a fifth starter. If they had realized he was right under their nose in Dunedin, Guzman may have had enough wins to beat out the the Twins' Chuck Knoblauch as American League rookie of the year. As it was, he finished second.

Guzman had turned to pitching in his native Santo Domingo when he was 13. Until then, he had been an outfielder, but took the mound because his team needed another arm to go along with their No. 1 hurler, boyhood pal Ramon Martinez, now with the Dodgers.

This time in Florida, Guzman, along with Morris and Winfield, was the centre of attention. Reporters liked what they heard from him almost as much as Pat Gillick did: "It's like I tell the little kids in the Dominican this year. I tell them base-

MICHAEL STUPARYK

CITO GASTON WATCHES HIS TROOPS GO THROUGH THEIR
PACES AT ENGLEBERT TRAINING COMPLEX.

ball's like school — the more you work, the more you learn. And I work hard, too. What I did last year was good but I don't want there to be just one year. I don't just want to be here two years; I want to be here a long time."

This time, there were no Guzman clones in camp, though rookie pitchers Pat Hentgen and Rick Trlicek showed enough to be brought north with the club when Stieb and hard-throwing middle reliever Mike Timlin went on the disabled list before the season began.

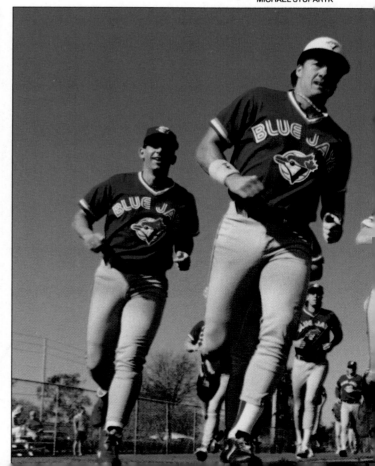

The other Jay in the spotlight, Dave Winfield, had an indifferent spring. First he had a sore back, worrisome for a 40-year-old who had missed the entire 1989 season following surgery to repair a herniated disk, the same injury that had laid Gaston and Stieb low last year. Then he tore a leg muscle and was unable to play for more than a week before the start of the season.

"I haven't been playing because I know if I get a hit, I'll want to run," Winfield told reporters. "And if I run, I might try to run too fast and blow it right out. And that could really set me back for weeks.

"It's a torn muscle and it has to heal. It's getting close and I'm being careful."

If anyone figured the wily veteran was saving himself for the season, they didn't say so out loud. But on opening day, guess who was ready to play — and to drive in the Jays' first run of the season.

Long before he showed he was still one of the great hitters in baseball, Winfield had been chalked in for 100 RBIs by new batting coach Larry Hisle, who knew a thing or two about hitting (28 homers and 119 RBIs for the Twins in '77 and 34 homers and 115 RBIs in '78). Hisle checked into camp with his arm in a sling, courtesy of a car mishap. He not only couldn't swing a bat but had to have his shoes laced by new first base coach Bob Bailor, the Jays' MVP in their opening season.

Hisle told a team meeting he also expected at least 100 RBIs from Carter, which comes with a money-back guarantee, and from Gruber, which doesn't. He also said he would improve Lee's hitting, which caused the odd titter in the clubhouse — but no one except Hisle is laughing any more.

Hisle, who is into statistics in a big way, realized he had a big job ahead of him. Despite finishing first in the East in '91, the Jays ranked 11th in both runs and RBIs and struck out 1,043 times — topped only by Cecil Fielder and his Tiger mates in Detroit.

Hisle replaced Gene Tenace, who moved to bench coach. Nobody knew what a bench coach did until late in the season when it became clear he was in charge of dirty looks.

Hitting improvement didn't come quickly, however. Right from Grapefruit Game One, against the Phils in Clearwater, the Jays lost a lot more than they won, often by one-sided scores. Morris started that first game, giving up a couple of runs in three innings in a 6-4 loss.

But then, Morris had been with the 1987 Tigers, who staged that furious stretch drive to nip the Jays for the AL East title despite going 9-20 in spring training. He didn't take the loss

MICHAEL STUPARYK

TRADER PAT GILLICK IS AN INTERESTED SPECTATOR AS THE TEAM HE ASSEMBLED GETS READY FOR THE SEASON.

GETTING IN SHAPE THE HARD WAY. DOING LAPS IS THE LEAST FUN OF ALL FOR JAYS IN TRAINING.

PATTI GOWER

too seriously.

"There's nothing tricky about what I'm trying to do here," he said. "I'm trying to get myself in shape and, obviously, there's a lot to be accomplished before opening day.

"For now, I'm still alive, the heart's still ticking and the sun will come up tomorrow. One of these days, the arm will come alive again, I'll have the smile on the face, the confidence will come back . . . it'll be a whole new ball game."

Anyway, the Jays put it together before a sellout crowd at Dunedin the next day to beat the White Sox 6-4, with Guzman putting in three scoreless innings and Kelly Gruber hitting a grand slam. Maybe the 1990 Gruber (31 homers, 118 RBIs) would show up this year instead of the 1991 edition (20 homers, 65 RBIs). At any rate, it looked as if Gaston's plans were to have Joe Carter hit third, with Winfield handling the cleanup spot and Gruber batting further down in the order than last year.

The spring schedule included back-to-back games with the Boston Red Sox, expected once again to supply the main opposition in the East by anyone who hadn't seen them play recently. The teams traded drubbings, with a much ballyhooed matchup between Roger Clemens and Morris turning out to be no contest. The new Toronto ace gave up four second-inning runs in an 11-4 shellacking at Winter Haven.

By the time the dust had settled beneath the palm trees, with a sidetrip to the Big O in Montreal for a two-game series against the Expos, the Jays were 13-18 in the spring, tied for 12th in the American League pre-season. But to show how little it meant, Texas had the best record of all (19-12) followed by the Orioles, who surely couldn't be taken seriously, or could they? Fans who worried about the sorry Grapefruit record were reminded that the 1991 Jays, who had won the AL East by seven games, were 9-19 in the spring.

Off to a really slow start in Florida was 23-year-old John Olerud, whose '91 season had been a bit of a disappointment, with a modest 17 homers and 68 RBIs. And why did the perfect swing that the club said would some day make him a superstar produce only a .256 batting average? Now it was spring, time for a new beginning, but it was 23 games into the Grapefruit League season before he produced an RBI, and that came when he was walked with the bases loaded.

Still, Olerud would be unlikely to get the Gruber treatment from the fans, no matter how slowly he came along. He was someone you wanted to cheer for, a guy for whom you readily offered the excuse that he had never played a game in the minors.

Just three years ago, Olerud had flirted with death, bringing home to all of us that even sports heroes are mortal. If there was a celluloid quality to the rest of the Jay cast, he at least was someone to whom we could all relate, someone out of the real world.

Olerud's health problems began in 1989, when he was a star athlete at Washington State University. He began to get such severe headaches that he could hardly bear the pain.

His doctor couldn't find the cause but when the lanky youngster finally collapsed one day, his physician father quickly sought a second opinion. This led to the discovery, near the base of Olerud's brain, of an aneurysm that had caused hemorrhaging into his spinal column. Life-saving surgery was done immediately.

Some people feel this brush with death accounts for the serenity that is so appealing in Olerud. He doesn't think so.

"I've always been that way, pretty calm," he says. "Baseball's a game where everyone's always saying you've got to stay on an even keel as much as you can, not get too excited, not get too upset. Maybe I'm a little bit too much on an even keel."

WAITING FOR HIS PITCH. WINFIELD SHOWS THE CONCENTRATION THAT HAS MADE HIM A STAR FOR NEARLY TWO DECADES.

MICHAEL STUPARYK

PATTI GOWER

ODD MAN OUT IN
TRAINING SESSION IS
PITCHER DAVE STIEB
WHO IS ON HIS OWN
RECOVERY PROGRAM
FROM OPERATION TO
REPAIR A HERNIATED
DISK.

KELLY GRUBER PINS
TRAINER TOMMY CRAIG
DURING TRAINING
HIJINKS AT ENGLEBERT
COMPLEX.

BY NEIL MacCARL

RAGS TO RICHES

In the beginning, they were the rag-tag Jays.

The year was 1977, the manager was Roy Hartsfield and the team was made up of kids and castoffs, plucked from the American League's expansion grab bag.

One of the skipper's first edicts, before that team ever took the field, had to do with looks. No shabby clothes. No facial hair below the lip.

Enter pitcher Pete Vuckovich, shaggy as a grizzly bear.

"Even Jesus Christ had long hair and a beard," Vuckovich said in his own defence, before the barber stopped by.

No, those early Jays weren't much to look at. The team, building for the future, loaded up with young guns in the expansion draft. Bob Bailor was the No. 1 draft choice and would go on to have a banner year, batting .310.

Bailor was one of a precious few on-field bright lights in that opening campaign. The season began in the middle of a spring snowfall, with 44,649 fans cooling their heels at Exhibition Stadium. Doug Ault warmed the fans' hearts with two homers in the opener.

More early-season excitement was provided by Otto (the Swatto) Velez, the American League's player of the month for April, and rookie lefthander Jerry Garvin, complete with high leg kick, tricky pickoff move and five wins in his first five decisions.

It was all downhill from there, with one stop on a Saturday afternoon in September. On that day, Roy Howell entered the Bronx Zoo and banged home nine runs, with two dingers and a pair of doubles, as the Jays thrashed the Yankees. Howell's nine RBIs are still the team standard.

The winning pitcher in that blowout, rookie Jim Clancy, got credit for his first shutout later that month — with a twist. Baltimore manager Earl Weaver yanked his team off the field at the Ex, because there was a tarpaulin on the bullpen mound and he thought it was a hazard. It went into the books as a 9-0 Jays triumph, one of 54 wins the team scratched out.

In '78, the Odd Couple — Big John Mayberry at first base and designated hitter Rico (Beeg Mon) Carty — stepped in to supply some heavy-duty lumber. There were plenty more moves to come, though, as general manager Pat Gillick began to establish a reputation as an astute, careful baseball mind. Newcomers included shortstop Alfredo Griffin (who would share rookie of the year honors with Twins third baseman John Castino in '79), second baseman Damaso Garcia (acquired from the Yankees) and first baseman Willie Upshaw (drafted in '78).

Gillick refused to shop for a quick fix on the free agent market. He poured time and money into stocking the farm system. Soon, a trickle of talent reached the big league club — Dave Stieb, an outfield prospect turned pitcher, followed by righthander Luis Leal and outfielder Lloyd (Shaker) Moseby.

Bobby Mattick took over from Hartsfield after the '79 season, but it was a long haul until '82, when

BORIS SPREMO

SNUGGLING UP FOR THE FRIGID 1977 HOME OPENER IN THE SNOW OF EXHIBITION STADIUM WERE JANET GUNN, LEFT, AND ALEXANDRA JULIAN.

manager Bobby Cox moved in for his first of four years at the helm.

The Jays were poised to move out of the cellar that year, and 78 wins matched Cleveland's total. It was a start.

In '83, Moseby became the first Jay to score 100 times in a season. Upshaw was the first to break the 100-RBI barrier. And George Bell arrived for a look-see. An 89-win campaign was good for fourth place. In '84, 89 wins was second only to the dreaded Tigers.

By '85, the club had in place an exciting, hard-hitting young outfield with power and speed to burn: Bell, Moseby and Jesse Barfield. On the mound, Stieb, Clancy, Jimmy Key and Doyle Alexander made for a solid starting staff.

In the bullpen, the Jays had paid big-time for righthander Bill Caudill and were looking for big results. They're still looking.

Seasoned lefty Gary Lavelle provided some relief, but the diamond in the rough was a stranger named Tom Henke. Gillick had picked up the Terminator from the Rangers as compensation for losing veteran DH Cliff Johnson. Henke supplied 13 saves down the stretch.

Add it all up and the Jays were AL East champions. It was on to the playoffs, where they took three of four from the West champion Kansas City Royals. But something hap-

GRAHAM BEZANT

INSTANT HERO IN '77 WAS FIRST BASEMAN DOUG AULT, ABOVE, SEEN SMACKING THE FIRST OF TWO HOMERS IN JAYS' FIRST GAME.

MEANWHILE, JACK BROHAMER OF THE WHITE SOX MADE THE BEST OF THE SNOWY CONDITIONS BY USING CATCHER'S PADS AS SNOW SHOES.

BORIS SPREMO

pened on the way to the World Series, and the Royals won in seven.

Out with Cox, in with Jimy (One M) Williams. Cox's decision to leave for the Atlanta Braves front office in '86 came as a surprise, and Williams struggled to make the new job his. The first of several squabbles began when Garcia was dropped from the leadoff spot in the batting order.

The Jays finished fourth in their 10th anniversary season, but '87 would bring more to cheer about.

Bell made the most noise — as he often did. His 47 homers and 134 RBIs established team records and earned American League MVP honors. Key was second in the Cy Young balloting with 17 wins. And the AL East crown seemed to be in the bag heading into the final days.

Seven straight season-ending losses changed that. With shortstop Tony Fernandez and catcher Ernie Whitt shelved by injuries, the Tigers won in a photo finish.

There were rumblings of discontent in the spring of '88. Williams wanted the league's MVP, Bell, to hand over his outfielder's glove and take a regular turn as designated hitter. The shakeup would also move the Shaker to left from his centre-field home.

Bell, sometimes referred to as the Butcher of San Pedro, wasn't hot on the idea. He was just hot. Bell sat out a spring training game, sparking a suspension. In mid-season another blowup, this time at the Metrodome. He sat out three games.

The line was drawn in the dirt. Bell predicted he'd outlast Williams — and he was right. In May of '89, Williams became the first Jays manager to be fired in mid-flight. His replacement? Hitting coach Cito Gaston.

The team responded to Gaston's low-key approach by winning the divisional title, going 77-49 after a 12-24 start. One of the spark plugs was a late arrival, Mookie Wilson, with his all-out all the time style of play.

The post-season was another disappointment, however. The Oakland Athletics, with Rickey (Hot Dog) Henderson swiping everything but the Jumbotron, ran the Jays out of town in five. Jose Canseco also made a lasting impression by crushing a home run into Bob Uecker territory at the Sky-Dome.

That season, May 28 to be exact, also marked the team's farewell performance at Exhibition Stadium, the worst ballpark in the majors. The team's new home was the high-tech SkyDome. Talk about a change.

Also saying so long was Whitt, the last of the Blue Jays originals. He was traded to Cox's Braves.

There was plenty to remember about the '90 season. Stieb, whose autobiography is entitled *Tomorrow I'll Be Perfect*, stopped flirting with no-hitters and nailed one down — on Sept. 2 in Cleveland.

On Dec. 5, Stand Pat Gillick lost a nickname by swinging one of the biggest deals in baseball history. Fernandez and slugger Fred McGriff were sent packing to San Diego for second baseman Robbie Alomar and outfielder Joe Carter. Days earlier, Gillick acquired centre fielder Devon White for Junior Felix and Luis Sojo. Last, but not least, the Jays lost Bell to the Cubs via free agency.

The shakeup made a quick impression. White became the best defensive centre fielder in team history. Alomar could become the most complete player the club has ever had: with the glove, with the bat, on the bases — and he can bunt, too. Carter has replaced Bell's numbers, minus the hassles.

Their on-field exploits were seen by a record-breaking bunch of baseball fanatics — again. The Jays broke the major league attendance mark for the second year in a row, and passed the 4 million mark (considered untouchable) on Oct. 2, while hosting the Angels.

One of the few downsides to the '91 season was a back problem that sidelined Stieb after just nine starts. Reinforcements came from Cleveland (knuckleballer Tom Candiotti) and the minors (rookie fireballer Juan Guzman).

Back woes also sidelined Gaston for much of the stretch drive. Hitting coach Gene Tenace took the reins for 33 games, until Gaston returned for the ride home.

Once again, the post-season was a disaster as the Jays were eliminated in five games by the Minnesota Twins, who swept three at the SkyDome and went on to win it all.

Those 4 million fans who flocked to the dome gave the Jays the financial firepower they needed to make two key moves for '92, landing righthander Jack Morris, a World Series hero with the Twins, and days later for 40-year-old slugger Dave Winfield.

GRAHAM BEZANT

FIRST PITCH IN TEAM HISTORY WAS THROWN BY BILL SINGER, A SORE-ARMED SLINGER WHO WENT 2-8 AND WAS GONE BY YEAR'S END

THE ORIGINALS

THIS WAS THE TEAM THAT TOOK THE FIELD AT EXHIBITION STADIUM FOR THAT HISTORIC APRIL 7, 1977, GAME. HOW MANY CAN YOU NAME WITHOUT LOOKING AT THE BOX BELOW?

First nine Jays were: (across top from left) right fielder Steve Bowling, shortstop Hector Torres, third baseman Dave McKay and first baseman Doug Ault; (immediately below them) left fielder John Scott and pitcher Bill Singer; DH Otto Velez and catcher Rick Cerone are below Scott and second baseman Pedro Garcia and centre fielder Gary Woods below Singer.

BLAST OFF

So, where were *you* that breezy Monday afternoon when it all began?

Listening to Tom and Jerry on a radio hidden in your desk at the office?

Playing hooky from school or work to watch on TV at home?

Or were you one of the lucky ones who drove to Tiger Stadium in the crisp, 9C sunshine to munch the world's best hot dogs, feast your eyes on a real grass playing field and witness the lift-off in person?

April 6, 1992. The day the Blue Jays finally took flight toward the World Series.

Remember? After 16 seasons of might-have-beens, there was a different feeling this opening day. A feeling shared by management, players and the rest of us that *THIS WAS IT*. Enough with the fond hopes. Enough with the shattered dreams and oh-so-close failures of this bunch some called the Blow Jays.

Here was a team with the highest payroll in the American League, and a lineup of talent that made it the pre-season favorite in all the experts' books.

No more excuses. It was time to produce. Time for these guys to go the distance.

And out there on the mound, scowling at those Tigers who'd been his teammates for 14 seasons, was the perfect man for the job — Mr. John Scott Morris.

Yes, Jack Morris was renowned for going the distance. Kinda had a thing about it. And today he was setting a major league record: 13 consecutive opening day starts.

Just a year before, he'd started the season for the Minnesota Twins. And 174 games later he'd finished it — with a magnificent 10-inning shutout of the Atlanta Braves for the World Series championship.

Now, Cactus Jack was poised to do it for us. Yes, for you and for me — and for $4.425 million.

Not that he was expected to do it alone. Hey, we had Dave Winfield on board — a future Hall of Famer signed for a mere $2.3 million to correct the team's chronic DH deficiency. (In '91, Toronto's DHs had produced an embarrassing five home runs and 56 RBIs — compared to the league average of 22 homers and 87 RBIs.)

Add to these an opening day lineup of Devon White, Roberto Alomar, Joe Carter, Kelly Gruber, John Olerud, Derek Bell, Pat Borders and Manny Lee and . . . well, how could you go wrong?

On this day, you couldn't.

Just take a glance at this first game, and you have a microcosm of what went so wonderfully right for the Jays of '92.

MIKE SLAUGHTER

CATCHER PAT BORDERS BACKS AWAY FROM LULU DIVINE AS SHE INVADES THE FIELD DURING THE FOURTH INNING OF THE JAYS' SEASON OPENER AT DETROIT. AFTER THEY DRAGGED LULU AWAY, BORDERS SMACKED A TWO-RUN HOMER.

INJURY-PLAGUED KELLY GRUBER STILL SHONE IN FIELD BUT WAS WOEFUL AT THE PLATE, BATTING .231 AND SMACKING ONLY EIGHT HOMERS IN THE FIRST HALF.

JEFF GOODE

In the first inning, before you could say "MVP," Alomar had ripped a double to left-centre, been advanced to third by Carter and scored on Winfield's first Blue Jays base hit.

It was a nightmarish scenario that opposing AL pitchers were to see many, many times this breakthrough year:

Alomar and/or White on base, Big Joe at the plate, and the 6-foot-6, 245-pound Winfield eagerly waiting on deck. That, my friends, is how you spell T-R-O-U-B-L-E.

Still, you can't win a pennant with half a lineup. The Jays had learned that the previous October, when the Twins whipped them in five games. Some batting averages from that humbling American League Championship Series: Lee (.125); Candy Maldonado (.100); Rance Mulliniks (.125); Olerud (.158).

But that was then; this was now, with the new, improved Borders and Olerud launching home runs as our heroes whipped the Tigers 4-2.

Oh, and let us not forget Cactus Jack. He went all the way, of course. Laughed at the boos. Threw 145 pitches. Not bad for a 36-year-old.

And not bad for a team that had lost eight of its last nine spring training games.

"Winning," a beaming Winfield concluded after his 3-for-4 day. "Winning the whole thing. That's the big motivation.

"This team's close. I got a gut feeling."

Uh-huh. And a lot of us felt good all over when Dave, Joe and the boys went on to sweep three from the Tigers before checking into the SkyDome to take on the team destined to be their most persistent East Division rival, the Baltimore Orioles.

Whew! That was some home opener, wasn't it?

Three big runs off Jimmy Key before many of the 50,424 witnesses had settled into their seats. But Gruber and Co. kept hacking until it was 3-2 Baltimore in the bottom of the ninth.

Which brings us once again to the rejuvenated Borders. POW! Home run off Orioles relief ace Gregg Olson.

Could this be the same Borders who'd gone hitless in his first 21 at-bats and hadn't homered until *July 30* in '91, leading the league with three? Aaaay, maybe that surprise on-field visit from the voluptuous Lulu Divine at the Detroit opener *did* make a difference.

Moments later, with White perched on second, Alomar lined an Olson curve into centre for the winning run.

Yeah! Even those irritating new SkyDome fireworks seemed tolerable after that.

As columnist Rosie DiManno chirped to Star readers the next day: *"How do you like 'em so far? New, improved and almost guaranteed not to fade."*

For a long time, they didn't.

After 15 games, they were 12-3, leading the surprising Yankees by 2½ games and the Orioles by three. The Red Sox, picked by many as the Jays' main rival, were flailing to stay afloat at 6-6.

Game No. 16 was a loss, in more ways than one.

Eleven painful months after a first base collision had left

ON OPENING DAY AT THE DOME, JIMMY KEY HELD

BALTIMORE TO THREE RUNS BUT LEFT ONE RUN DOWN.

28

RON BULL

FIRST PITCHES OPENING DAY WERE THROWN OUT BY
ROBERTA BONDAR AND KERRIN LEE-GARTNER.

CELEBRATION TIME. JOE CARTER CONGRATULATES DEVON
WHITE AFTER HE SCORES THE WINNING RUN IN THE NINTH
INNING OF THE SKYDOME OPENER.

him unable to bend over and pull on his socks, and four months after back surgery, Dave Stieb made his '92 debut.

The SkyDome crowd stood and cheered the club's first homegrown superstar — the kid-turned-vet who, after 14 years of tantrums, frustration and brilliance, ranked as our longest-serving performer. A touchstone with the past.

Even his bullpen buddies donned shoulder-length, Stieb-style hairpieces and bowed in mock supplication.

But the Cleveland Indians were not so friendly to the Jays' career leader in wins (174), strikeouts (1,631) and no-hitters (one). After six so-so innings and four earned runs, the erstwhile ace was outta there.

"It wasn't a total disaster," he said later, "but there's plenty of work to do."

But work didn't help. What his peers had called the league's best slider had lost its snap, and the fastball wasn't so fast. By July, Stieb had been bumped to the bullpen by rookie starters Doug Linton and Pat Hentgen. His ERA was over

five, and he had a painful new problem: tendinitis in the elbow.

Fortunately, there were other arms to carry the load.

When free-agent knuckleballer Tom Candiotti took his lucrative hike to the Los Angeles Dodgers in the off-season, there were concerns. But, with the addition of Morris, the '92 staff looked *better* than the mound corps that had led the AL in '91 with 91 wins and a 3.50 ERA.

Morris, Key, Juan Guzman, Todd Stottlemyre, with David Cone lurking over the horizon. Backed by Tom Henke, Duane Ward, David Wells and the deepest bullpen in baseball. Not bad.

By mid-May, Jays pitching ranked third in the AL with a nifty 3.38 ERA. But Baltimore's was only 2.99, which explains why they trailed by only 1½ games.

In hitting, the Jays also ranked third at .265, trailing the Twins by 20 points.

Ah, those Twins. They certainly had our number in '91. And it looked like the same old script when the inter-divisional rivals renewed hostilities at the SkyDome, May 18 to 20.

For starters, the ingrates beat Morris, the gun-for-hire free agent who'd bestowed his favors on them the year before. Without Jack, they wouldn't be wearing those World Series rings. The next night, Kirby Puckett and his cronies pounced on Stieb with hoarse animal cries, administering a 7-1 thrashing.

But the next night . . . now *that* was a rumble to remember.

Corked bats, beanballs, bench-jockey hijinx, on-field melees — even a one-man search-and-destroy mission.

It all began when light-hitting Twins shortstop Greg Gagne lined a two-run homer off Stottlemyre.

Then, before you could say "Donnybrook," the Jays bench was yelling about corked bats, Twins manager Tom Kelly was heckling the sainted Alomar, Scowling Scott Erickson was throwing fastballs *behind* Derek Bell, and . . .

COLIN McCONNELL

DONNING STIEB-LIKE WIGS, HIS BULLPEN BUDDIES WELCOME THE FORMER ACE OF THE STAFF BACK FOR HIS FIRST START AT SKYDOME ON APRIL 22. HE GAVE UP FOUR RUNS IN SIX INNINGS AND CAME OUT ON THE WRONG END OF A 7-2 SCORE. TEAMMATES SAY HIS HAIR LOOKS LIKE THE MOSS THAN HANGS DOWN FROM FLORIDA LIVE OAKS.

GOODBYE BASEBALL! STIEB WATCHES FIRST-INNING SMASH BY FORMER TEAMMATE GLENALLEN HILL SAIL OVER THE WALL.

PATTI GOWER

Holy kamikaze! Stottlemyre was charging the Twins dugout singlehanded, taking on all comers.

Well, they eventually got the boys settled down without bloodshed. Stottlemyre was gone, and the Twins were leading 6-2 after four. But then some other interesting things happened.

The slumping Gruber, forgetting his aches and pains in the emotion of it all, blasted a homer to left. Then White and Alomar got aboard, and you could see Winfield was itching to get up there and drive them home.

Well, he didn't have to. Carter, looking as intense and focused as a tomcat stalking a chickadee, sent an Erickson fastball d-e-e-e-p into the second deck. It was 6-6.

Thereafter, there was a sense of inevitability about it all, as the rookie Bell's first major league homer and key singles by Olerud and Borders produced an 8-7, 10-inning victory.

"The ruckus sure didn't hurt," closer Tom Henke drawled. "We've got a lot of pride and we want to win."

The Curse of the Twins was broken. From there, the Jays dominated Minnesota 6-3, including a 16-5 drubbing in September for Cone's first AL win.

And what of the Jays' traditional East Division nemesis, the Red Sox?

Six weeks into the season, the Olde Towne Team simply looked olde. Slugger Jack Clark, facing personal bankruptcy despite his $8.7 million, three-year contract, was suddenly bankrupt at the plate, hitting .190.

Lefty starter Matt Young, who somehow contrived to hurl an April no-hitter against Cleveland and *lose*, was a $6.3 million joke destined for bullpen mopup duties.

Wade Boggs, a career .381 hitter at Fenway, was struggling to stay above .250. And outfielder Phil Plantier, who'd raised great expectations with 11 homers in only 148 at-bats the year before, was whiffing along at a .230 clip with no power, writing himself a ticket to Pawtucket.

Top-of-the-line outfielders Mike Greenwell (bad leg) and Ellis Burks (bad back) were destined for the disabled list, where first baseman Carlos Quintana already languished via an off-season car crash in Venezuela.

Sure, Roger Clemens was great, and free-agent refugee Frank Viola was decent. But the sockless Sox, with the

30

league's second-highest payroll at $42,203,584 (the Jays were tops at $42,663,666), were suffering a shocking power outage (11 home runs in mid-May, compared to 49 for Detroit) and riding an express elevator to the basement.

Meanwhile, on the up car, everybody had to make room for the Orioles.

Could this possibly be the team that had lost 95 games in '91, finishing 24 lengths behind the Blue Jays in sixth place? Nooo way.

You see, those fledgling birds from Baltimore had the worst pitching in the majors last year with a 4.59 ERA. But with a blossoming Mike Mussina, a rejuvenated Rick Sutcliffe and a maturing Ben McDonald in the starting rotation, backed by the stingy Olson and Gomer Pyle looka-like Todd Frohwirth in the bullpen, the Orioles boasted the league's *best* pitching after six weeks.

Having catcher Chris Hoiles hitting a lusty .327 and out-of-nowhere outfielder Brady Anderson vying for the league lead in RBIs, stolen bases, runs and hits didn't hurt, either. Not to mention blue-ribbon years for third baseman Leo Gomez and outfielder Mike Devereaux.

Okay, so Cal Ripken wasn't matching his MVP numbers of '91 (.323, 34 homers, 114 RBIs), but he was still the best offensive shortstop this side of Ernie Banks.

The Milwaukee Brewers? Who's worried about those perennial also-rans who'd finished fourth last year?

Wasn't one of their most promising pitchers, sidearming righty Julio (Iguana Man) Machado, in a Venezuelan jail after admitting he was the triggerman in a fatal shooting?

Weren't they missing ace lefty Teddy Higuera again? And wasn't shortstop Bill Spiers gone for the season after back surgery?

Did they really expect to win with Kansas City Royals cast-off Kevin Seitzer at third? And who was this guy Pat Listach?

Ahem. More on these upstarts later.

Anyway, starting with that breezy Monday in Detroit and cruising through a sensational 16-7 April, a so-so 15-12 May and a mediocre 14-12 June before surging in July, our heroes checked into the all-star break at 53-34, one game ahead of their '91 pace.

Sure, they were four games ahead of the Orioles, 7½ ahead of the Brewers and 10 over Boston, and yet . . .

There was still a feeling of *underachievement* here. Like getting behind the wheel of a Rolls-Royce and discovering you

RICHARD LAUTENS

CHARGING THE MOUND AFTER BEING HIT BY A PITCH FROM BREWERS' JAIME NAVARRO (RIGHT), JOE CARTER STARTED A BENCH-CLEARING BRAWL IN MAY 27 GAME AT SKYDOME.

FIGHTING MAD, PITCHER TODD STOTTLEMYRE IS RESTRAINED BY UMPIRE LARRY YOUNG DURING A TESTY SKYDOME GAME AGAINST THE TWINS. STOTTLEMYRE OBJECTED TO PITCHER SCOTT ERICKSON THROWING BEHIND DEREK BELL AFTER BEING TAGGED FOR A HOMER. JAYS WON GAME 8-7.

TONY BOCK

RON BULL

had a lawnmower engine under the hood. It might get you there. But where was the surge of power?

And where was Kelly Gruber?

"Yo, Groobah! How's that hangnail?" SkyDome hecklers shouted.

They had a point. Here was a guy who'd been voted Toronto's most popular athlete in a Star poll less than two years ago. And why not? The 1990 Blue Jays player of the year had hit a solid .274 with 31 homers and 118 RBIs while playing a Gold Glove third base. No wonder he was named to three all-star teams.

Now, after a sub-par '91 in which he'd missed 49 games because of lingering injuries, Gruber had led the team in Grapefruit League homers and RBIs. He was expected to be a force.

Instead, he was a farce. Complaining about mysterious stiff necks, bum knees and aching shoulders, Gruber missed 38 of the first 107 games and was hitting a squishy-soft .231 at the break.

Was this the same guy who'd been labelled "One tough Blue Jay" as cover boy of the 1990 edition of Bill Mazeroski's baseball annual?

Now that he was earning more than $20,000 a game, had the ex-footballer lowered his pain threshold to basement level?

Nobody would say exactly what the problems were, or how long they would last. Exasperated with reporters' questions, manager Cito Gaston sighed: "I don't even wanna talk about the guy."

And there were other first-half disappointments:

Bell, minor league player of the year (.346 at Syracuse), cracked two hits in the season opener, then cracked a bone in his hand the next day. Out for a month, he lost his job to Maldonado.

Reliever Mike Timlin, a pleasant surprise in '91, began the season on the DL with a sore elbow, couldn't join the Jays until mid-June and was hit hard.

Stottlemyre, who'd won 15 last year, struggled with his control and emotions. Like Stieb, he finished the first half with a losing record and an ERA over five.

Still, with some big guys named Alomar, Carter, Winfield, Morris, Guzman, Ward and Henke doing the job (more on them later), and some hidden treasures named Manuel Lee and Jeff Kent coming through, the Blue Jays entered the second half on top.

They were still the team to beat.

BERNARD WEIL

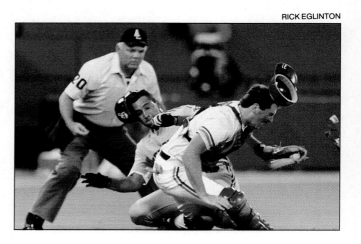

RICK EGLINTON

TOP: DOUBLE TROUBLE, CAL AND BILLY RIPKEN DURING APRIL 12 SKYDOME VISIT.

MIDDLE: TOUGH BREAK FOR DEREK BELL AS HE CRACKS BONE IN HIS HAND APRIL 10.

BOTTOM: CRUNCH TIME FOR CATCHER GREG MYERS IN COLLISION AT PLATE APRIL 22.

TONY BOCK

BEST MOMENT OF '92 FOR KELLY GRUBER CAME IN A MAY 31 GAME AT SKYDOME AGAINST THE WHITE SOX. WITH THE GAME TIED IN THE NINTH, HE DOUBLED AGAINST RELIEVER BOBBY THIGPEN AND SCORED FROM SECOND WITH A HEAD-FIRST SLIDE. HE RAISES HIS HAND IN VICTORY AS UMPIRE TIM WELKE CALLS HIM SAFE. ODDLY ENOUGH, CATCHER RON KARKOVICE, INSERTED FOR DEFENSIVE PURPOSES LATE IN THE GAME, MADE NO ATTEMPT AT BLOCKING THE PLATE.

PICK OF THE JAYS

The Blue Jays had something new at the 1992 All-Star Game in San Diego, but something old was missing.

Juan Guzman, sporting an 11-2 first-half record and a sparkling 2.11 ERA in his first full major league season at age 25, was named to the American League all-star cast of hurlers by Minnesota manager Tom Kelly, but 40-year-old Dave Winfield failed to make the team despite a spectacular opening half.

"I earned a spot and it didn't happen," said Winfield, who had played in 12 consecutive all-star contests before a herniated disk put him out of action for the entire 1989 season.

His first-half stats (.303 average, 14 homers and 47 RBIs) were good enough for the fans, but not for Kelly. The card-punchers had made Winfield their No. 4 outfield pick behind Oakland's Jose Canseco, Minnesota's Kirby Puckett and Seattle's Ken Griffey Jr. They had picked Joe Carter No. 5.

So, with Canseco on the disabled list, Winfield figured he would get the call. But Kelly opted for Joltin' Joe (.280 average, 19 homers and 62 RBIs) instead, largely because there would be no designated hitter in this National League park affair.

"I think he deserved to go," Carter said of Winfield. "He's been there all year for us, but I've only been hot for a month and a half."

Despite the fact that the SkyDome attracts a record number of fans, the only Jay to garner enough votes to make it as a starter was second baseman Roberto Alomar, chosen first for the second straight year.

Orioles shortstop Cal Ripken Jr. received the most votes,

BERNARD WEIL

SAN DIEGO BOUND FOR THE ALL-STAR GAME, JUAN GUZMAN AND JOE CARTER CONGRATULATE THEMSELVES ON HEARING THE NEWS.

JEFF GOODE

2,699,733. Other members of the AL starting lineup were Puckett and Griffey, Mark McGwire of the Athletics at first base, Wade Boggs of the Red Sox at third and Alomar's brother, Sandy, behind the plate.

A pre-game poll of managers revealed they disagreed with the fans on four AL picks. The managers would have replaced Boggs with Chicago's Robin Ventura, Sandy Alomar with Detroit's Mickey Tettleton, and Canseco and Griffey with Carter and Brady Anderson, who was in the midst of a sensational season with the Orioles — as the Jays could testify.

Just as well the managers didn't have their way. It might have been an even greater slaughter at Jack Murphy Stadium, where the AL dished out a 16-6 drubbing of the Nationals for their fifth consecutive all-star victory.

Guzman was ecstatic about his selection.

"The way I've been pitching, I deserve it," he said in his refreshingly candid way. He recalled watching the All-Star Game on TV in the Dominican Republic and dreaming of some day being there. "It's unbelievable. All my hard work has paid off. I feel proud of myself and happy."

The NL team was led by Cubs second baseman Ryne Sandberg, top selection for the second straight year with 2,785,407 votes. Former Jay Fred McGriff of the Padres was picked at first, while teammates Benito Santiago (catcher) and Tony Gwynn (outfielder) were also chosen by the fans. The other NL starters were: outfielders Andy Van Slyke and Barry Bonds of Pittsburgh; third baseman Terry Pendleton of Atlanta; and Ozzie Smith of St. Louis at short. But they proved no match for the powerful AL club, which smashed a record 19 hits, including one by pitcher Charles Nagy of Cleveland, batting for the first time in '92.

Returning to San Diego for the first time since their trade, Carter and Alomar showed they had lost none of their magic before 59,372 fans. Carter, making his second straight all-star

PLAYS LIKE THIS SENT A HAPPY ROBBIE ALOMAR TO THE ALL-STAR GAME AS THE FANS' SELECTION FOR THE SECOND YEAR IN A ROW.

LEFT AT HOME WAS DAVE WINFIELD, DESPITE THE FACT HE GOT THE FOURTH-MOST VOTES AMONG OUTFIELDERS.

appearance, had two hits, an RBI and scored a run while improving his all-star batting average to .750. Alomar became the first all-star to steal two bases in a single inning when he swiped second and third in the second, after smacking his first all-star hit.

The other Jay, Guzman, lost the starting assignment to Kevin Brown of Texas, then came on in the third inning and put in one Guzman of an inning. He blew Sandberg and Santiago away to start, then loaded the bases before getting Bonds to pop up. Twenty-five pitches, but no damage, except to manager Kelly's nerves.

Griffey — who had three hits, including a homer — was the most valuable player.

One oddity: Six players involved in recent Jays trades, three on each side, made an appearance: Carter, Alomar and Guzman for the AL; McGriff, Tony Fernandez and Mike Sharperson (acquired by the Dodgers in exchange for Guzman) for the NL.

BIRD DOGGED

Looking back, it's tempting to call it Fate.

It was simply the Blue Jays' year, you see. Our boys had it all the way.

The Team of Destiny, overcoming all obstacles to march resolutely to the inevitable triumph.

Yeah. *Riiight!*

You didn't hear too much of that kind of talk around T.O the morning of Thursday, Aug. 13.

It was another miserable day in Southern Ontario. Cool and wet. As it had been so often this non-summer of 17 consecutive rainy weekends.

But it wasn't just the weather that had us down. It was those upstart Orioles.

They'd just trashed our heroes two straight at SkyDome, and the ominous headline in The Star read: **JUST ONE.**

Three-quarters of the season gone, and *just one game* separated the Jays and their most persistent pursuers atop the American League East.

What had gone wrong with the Team of Destiny?

You could start with Juan Guzman.

Just 10 days before, Juanderful Juan ranked as the Jay's stopper — the intimidating fireballer with the star-spangled 12-2 record who ranked third in the AL in strikeouts, ERA and winning percentage.

When he took the mound against Roger Clemens at Fenway Park Aug. 3, the game was billed as a titanic matchup.

But for Guzman it was more like the voyage of the Titanic. The Red Sox pounded him for six runs in four innings, including an audacious steal of home by Billy Hatcher.

But the biggest shock occurred during a mound conference before Guzman's departure. Why was manager Cito Gaston wagging his finger at Juan like an exasperated teacher scolding a schoolboy?

Star baseball columnist Dave Perkins reported there were two versions of the story:

One, that Cito was upset by Guzman's failure to brush back Wade Boggs in retaliation for a too-close-for-comfort Clemens' fastball over Pat Borders' head.

And two, that Cito was upset because Guzman had ignored his signal for a change-up to Boggs.

As it turned out, there was good reason for the taciturn Dominican's reluctance to throw off-speed stuff. He'd missed his previous start due to a sore shoulder, and now the pain was back. Change-ups produced the worst twinges.

Two days later, Guzman was on the disabled list.

Which seemed to be the signal for a total pitching collapse. Here's how Jay starters fared the

RICK EGLINTON

TOO LATE: PAT BORDERS HAS THE PLATE BLOCKED NEATLY BUT CANDY MALDONADO'S THROW IS TOO LATE TO NAB THE YANKEES' RANDY VELARDE. JAYS WON THIS AUG. 2 SKYDOME SQUEAKER 7-6 ON A JOE CARTER HOME RUN.

RON BULL

ABOVE: JUAN GUZMAN MAKES A POINT ON RETURN FROM DL.

next five games:
David Wells: 8 runs in 5 innings.
Jack Morris: 6 runs in 5.
Todd Stottlemyre: 4 runs in 2⅔.
Dave Stieb: 5 runs in 3.
Jimmy Key: 7 runs in 5⅔.

Is all that bad stuff coming back to you now? Then you undoubtedly remember that damp Thursday when one more win could flutter the Orioles up to share the Jays' league-leading perch.

All that stood in their way was a 27-year-old "kid" just up from Syracuse making (gulp) his first big league start — Doug Linton.

Remember that afternoon? The incredible Silken Laumann, fresh from her own personal triumph and Canada's Olympic success story in Barcelona, threw out the first pitch.

The next 101 pitches were thrown by Linton, who limited the Orioles to three hits over eight innings.

Tom Henke finished up for his 21st save, and the Blue Jays were back on top by two.

Biggest win of the season, some said.

"Well, yeah. It was pretty important," a beaming Gaston agreed. "You go from a possible tie for first to two games up. It was just such a lift for all of us."

Especially for Cito, who needed all the lifts he could get.

For a long time — particularly since the Jays' embarrassing loss to the Twins in the 1991 League Championship Series —

BELOW: ORIOLES CELEBRATE BLOWING AWAY JAYS ON AUG. 12

BERNARD WEIL

COLIN McCONNELL

CANDY MALDONADO DRIVES IN DAVE WINFIELD WITH SMASH TO LEFT AGAINST THE YANKS.

critics had been claiming the team's weakest position was manager.

After the ALCS debacle, CBS baseball analyst Jim Kaat had put it this way: "The Blue Jays were out-pitched, out-played and out-managed."

Cito-bashing had become the most popular game in town on sports radio call-in shows.

"Why does Cito keep playing Candy Maldonado in left when he's only hitting .217?" they yammered in early June.

Because Cito had faith that the veteran would come around, just as he had the year before. Cito was right. Candy wound up hitting .270-plus with with good power and RBI totals for a No. 6 hitter.

He showed the same sort of faith when he predicted Manuel Lee could be an everyday shortstop, and that John Olerud would snap out of his early-season doldrums.

"Why doesn't Cito show more emotion? Why doesn't he get mad, bawl out the players?"

Mostly, Cito ignored such questions. But here's what he told Star columnist Milt Dunnell:

"I was a player. And I like to think of myself as a player's manager. I'm not demonstrative. And I'm not handling people from ordinary walks of life. These guys are specialists and they're making more money than their employer.

"I'm not one to hold meetings and chew out the whole team because two or three guys are screwing up. As a player, I resented that. I call the two or three into my office and chew them out."

Why doesn't Cito show a little imagination? Call the double-steal, initiate some trick plays, juggle the lineup?

What you see is what you get with Cito. He likes a set line-up, doesn't feel he has to resort to razzle-dazzle with this team.

And it didn't work out too badly, did it? True, the one-time batting coach was no whiz at handling pitchers. But in the American League, only Tony La Russa has won more games in the past three seasons.

So Cito was smiling that Thursday afternoon after Linton's 4-2 win (a game in which the maligned Maldonado got two hits and drove in a big run). But there was more trouble ahead.

No sooner had Baltimore been slapped down than Milwaukee began to get uppity. The Brewers, who began the season with more lifetime victories against Toronto than any other club (114-82), brought Doug Linton back to earth with a thud.

Just a week after his SkyDome heroics, Linton was hammered for eight runs in three innings at County Stadium. During his next two appearances he would give up 11 more earned runs in two innings.

Wait, it gets worse. That was only a warm-up for the savagery inflicted on David Wells next afternoon. After 4⅓ shell-shocked innings, the San Diego Doughboy had yielded 11 hits and 13 earned runs — the worst shellacking in team history.

And now the Brewers were just 4½ games back.

Not that it was *all* bad news.

At the SkyDome, fans were on their way to breaking the all-time major league attendance record they'd set the year before (4,001,526). And why not? they were seeing entertaining, sound baseball at almost every position.

Behind the plate, Pat Borders had clearly established himself as the everyday catcher, relegating Greg Myers to the bench, then to California in a trade for reliever Mark Eichhorn.

By mid-season, Borders was on a pace to call more games than any other American League catcher this season and had hit more homers (seven compared to five) than he'd managed all last year. (What happened to all that talk of trading him to San Diego for Benito Santiago?).

At first base, Olerud still caused jitters with his glove. (Remember that May 18 loss to the Twins, when Duane Ward unleashed a pickoff throw while Olerud was having a little chat with Kirby Puckett at first? The missile whizzed past the unsuspecting Olerud's head — enabling Puckett to go to third

BERNARD WEIL

GOOD LUCK SIGN! ROBBIE ALOMAR SIGNS BALL FOR OLYMPIC ROWING STAR SILKEN LAUMANN THEN DRIVES IN WINNING RUN AUG. 13 AGAINST ORIOLES.

and eventually score the winning run).

But, after a slow start, there was nothing wrong with Olerud's bat. By mid-September, he was flirting with .300, with 15 homers and 60 RBI.

At second, Roberto Alomar was having his finest season: Fielding his position like the all-star he was, ranking with the league leaders in hitting, and demonstrating every day that sports heros *can* be caring, balanced, happy human beings.

At short, Lee was the most pleasant surprise of all. Pathetic in '91 when he attempted to replace fan favorite Tony Fernandez with a .234 average, 29 RBI and 107 strikeouts, Lee became an object of ridicule when Jays signed him to a $1 million contract for '92.

Expected to lose his job to Eddie Zosky in spring training, Lee rose to the challenge, enjoyed his best year in the field and at the plate, and won the fans' respect. Once again, Cito's glacial-paced patience had paid off.

At third, Kelly Gruber was a huge disappointment for a second consecutive season. But how about that Jeff Kent?

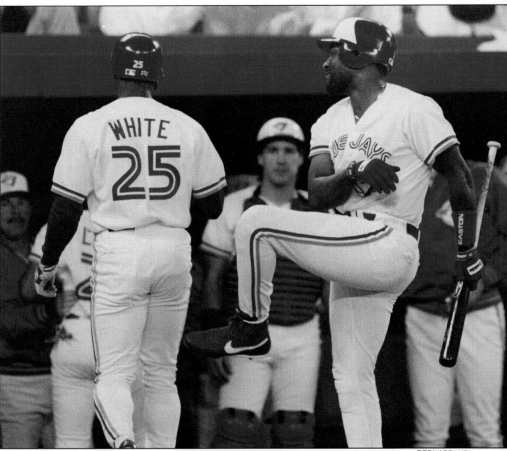

BERNARD WEIL

JOE GETS A KICK OUT OF DEVON AFTER WHITE SCORES IN AUG. 13 WIN OVER ORIOLES

Just two seasons after hitting a mere .244 for St. Catharines in the Rookie League, the cheerful California Beach Boy quickly became the SkyDome banner-bearers' favorite pin-up.

With the injury-prone Gruber out so often, Kent was able to step right up from Syracuse and drive in big runs with the best of them. With 28 RBI in 158 at-bats by early August, Kent's production ratio was right up there with Joe Carter's — and far better than Gruber's.

Good luck with the Mets, kid. We hated to see you go.

In left field, Maldonado was expected to be rookie phenom Derek Bell's caddy. But when Bell got hurt, then struggled to get his stroke back, Candy took over and came through with a solid season.

In centre, Devon White's offensive numbers were down somewhat from his outstanding '91 season. And purists will tell you his on-base percentage isn't good enough for a leadoff hitter.

But ask any Toronto pitcher to name their favorite Blue Jay, and it has to be man with the Golden Glove. After years of watching those liners, pops and gappers elude the likes of Mookie Wilson and George Bell, it was pure joy to see the Big Glider make defence look so easy.

And in right, Joe Carter just kept on doing it, didn't he? The man who'd averaged 30 home runs and 109 RBI for the previous six seasons came through with another big one: 30-plus homers and 115-plus RBI. Hustling, smiling and boosting his mates every step of the way.

So who does that leave among the regulars?

Ooooooh, yeah. The DH. Mr. David Mark Winfield. The guy the California Angels considered too old.

He *was* old, in baseball years. Oldest player to hit three homers in one game. Oldest player to hit for the cycle.

And in this incredible year, destined to be the only 40-year-old to ever drive in 100 runs.

As August wound down and the Blue Jays approached the stretch drive, you had to ask yourself: Where would they be without Winfield?

Still, despite Winfield's heroics, Guzman's successful return from the disabled list the day before and Stottlemyre's one-hitter against the White Sox a week earlier, everyone knew there was a l-o-n-g tough way to go.

Even as the cheers erupted for Winfield, memories lingered from just three nights earlier, when Milwaukee had raked Blue Jay pitching for a record 31 hits in the infamous 22-2 Friday Night Massacre.

Quite a how-do-you-do for the newest member of the team, who'd arrived just in time to witness the slaughter.

Blue Jay friends and foes were to see a lot of this newcomer in the critical weeks to come.

His name was David Cone.

KENT GOES AND THE
CONEHEADS ARRIVE.
JEFF KENT (SHOWN
TAGGING OUT YANKEES'
ANDY STANKIEWICZ IN A
3-1 WIN AUG. 2) WAS
TRADED TO METS WITH
ONLY 34 GAMES LEFT IN
SEASON TO OBTAIN
FIREBALLER DAVID CONE.
HIS OTHER-WORLDLY
FAN CLUB WAS THERE
FOR ALL CONE
OUTINGS.

SHADOW DANCING

It's late and you want to get home. Behind, you hear footsteps.

You look back and two shadows are following, one a little ahead of the other.

When you stop, they stop. When you speed up, they speed up.

No matter what you do, they are always there.

Finally, you outdistance the closest shadow. But now the other one has taken its place.

You run as hard as you can, but you can't shake it. It comes closer, CLOSER until . . .

Ever had that feeling?

Then you know exactly how the Blue Jays felt in September.

Like Dr. Richard Kimble in *The Fugitive,* or the haunted Jean Valjean in *Les Miserables,* the Jays were the quarry, pursued by two relentless predators called the Baltimore Orioles and Milwaukee Brewers.

For the longest time, commencing around apple blossom season in May, the closest shadow was cast by the Orioles — winning when the Jays did, losing when they faltered.

Now it was September, and the blossoms of May had become ripe apples ready for picking. Just like the American League East championship.

The evening of Wednesday, Sept. 2, was a delightful night for baseball at the SkyDome: roof open, no clouds, 18C. A perfect setting for a gut-grinding pitchers duel between Jimmy Key and Greg Hibbard of the White Sox.

With the Orioles just 1½ games back, the Jays need this one. With two on and two out, it seems they have it. Robbie Alomar has just slashed a sinking liner into right field. Extra bases, for sure!

Here comes Sox outfielder Mike Huff pumping hard toward the line. No way he can reach it. The tying run is coming home. Huff dives. Glove hand s-t-r-e-t-c-h-e-d. He tumbles. He rolls. Holds up his glove.

OMIGOD! He caught it! In the stands, 50,419 groan.

That was it, a 3-2 loss, combined with a 2-1 Orioles victory over Oakland to complete Baltimore's first sweep of the Athletics in five years.

After 134 games, the relentless Orioles are half a game back.

How d'ya like them apples?

Dave Winfield didn't like 'em one bit. So, the day after that loss to the White Sox, he gave a pep talk. To us, the fans.

"Wake up and cheer us on," roared The Star's page one banner headline on Sept. 3.

"The fans need us and we need them," Winfield told columnist Jim Proudfoot. "This is a symbiotic relationship. We feed off each other."

TONY BOCK

Toronto fans had heard this for years: They were too sedate; didn't know when to cheer; didn't really understand the game.

The last guy to tell us this had been Kelly Gruber, appealing in late May for the fans to get behind the team and lay off the boos. Unfortunately, Gruber's own performance (for which he received $3.6 million this year) seldom deserved cheers, and his appeal was quickly forgotten.

But when Winfield the future

**FANS RESPONDED WHEN
DAVE WINFIELD TOLD
THEM THEY NEEDED TO
SHOW THEIR SUPPORT
MORE STRONGLY DOWN
THE STRETCH.**

Hall of Famer spoke, we listened and we cheered.

"Winfield wants noise!" SkyDome banners screamed the next night. And darned if our heroes didn't go out and clobber the Twins 16-5.

Those cheers carried a long way — clear down to Kansas City and Texas, as Dave and the boys went on the road and won eight of 10 while Baltimore slipped to 4-6. Returning to the SkyDome on Sept. 14, the Jays led the Orioles by five games, the Brewers by six.

Not that anyone was relaxing. After 1987, no Toronto baseball fan could ever relax in September until the magic number was zero.

Ah, yes, 1987. Close your eyes, bite your knuckles and it all comes flooding back . . .

Tony Fernandez breaking his elbow. Ernie Whitt cracking his ribs. Leading the Tigers by 3½ with just six games to go.

Then losing three one-run games to Milwaukee at Exhibition Stadium. On to Detroit with a one-game lead and three to play. Two tough one-run defeats setting up the final game.

Jimmy Key pitching his heart out. One lazy, wind-blown Larry Herndon fly ball to left field. Back . . . back . . . juuust over the fence.

Frank Tanana smirking while teammates pour champagne over his head. "Hey, I just threw the ball up there. I dunno why they didn't hit it." Ninety-six wins and no cigar.

Okay, snap out of it! That was five years ago. Since then, the Jays had won the division twice (by two games over Baltimore in '89, and seven over Boston and Detroit in '91) and finished second twice (to Boston in '88 and '90).

And here they had a chance to repeat, as long as they could elude those pursuing shadows . . .

Going into a weekend series against Texas at the dome on Sept. 18, the Jays led Baltimore by three games and Milwau-

IF LOOKS COULD KILL, BATTERS WOULD DROP LIKE FLIES EVERY TIME JACK MORRIS PITCHES. THIS IS THE LOOK BALTIMORE GOT WHEN MORRIS FAILED IN AN EARLY ATTEMPT TO WIN HIS 20TH.

"WHAT DO I HAVE TO DO TO WIN?" JUAN GUZMAN SEEMS TO BE ASKING AFTER DROPPING A 2-1 DECISION TO THE YANKS ON SEPT. 26.

FOUNTAIN-OF-YOUTH SMILE FROM WINFIELD AFTER HE BECOMES THE FIRST PLAYER OVER 40 TO DRIVE IN 100 RUNS.

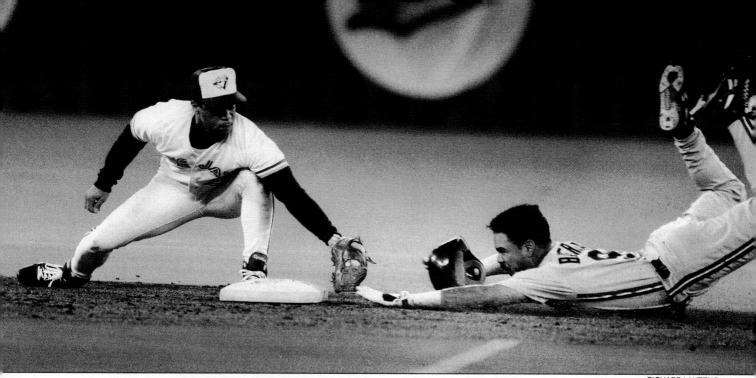

DEAD ON ARRIVAL. ROBBIE ALOMAR TAGS OUT HIS MAIN RIVAL FOR TOP SECOND BASEMAN HONORS, CARLOS BAERGA OF THE INDIANS, IN SEPT. 16 GAME AT THE DOME.

TWIN KILLING IN PROGRESS. ALFREDO GRIFFIN LEAPS OVER KENT HRBEK TO COMPLETE DOUBLE PLAY AGAINST THE TWINS.

NICE TRY, NO CIGAR. KELLY GRUBER LUNGES FOR A BALL IN SEPT. 6 GAME BUT COMES UP EMPTY.

kee by five. Their magic number was 14.

Just two days later, Baltimore trailed by 5½, Milwaukee had moved into second place and the Jays' magic number had shrunk to nine. How could this happen?

What? Have you forgotten already? Through a delightful quirk of scheduling, the Jays' two main rivals were pitted *against each other* for seven critical games in mid-September.

When Baltimore lost 4-1 to the surging Brewers on Sept. 19, it marked the first time since April 28 that those *other* birds had not been first or second. Thereafter, it was a slide to destruction for the Orioles as they went 0-for-Milwaukee, lost nine of 13 and endured a streak of 125 innings in which they failed to score more than twice in one frame.

When Toronto took two of three in the long-awaited showdown at Baltimore's beautiful new Camden Yards, Sept. 22 to 24, there was a sense of anti-climax. Shockingly, it was all over for the Orioles. They were out of the race without a hope of even finishing second.

The implacable Brewers had taken that spot, with firm plans to move up. Sweeping Baltimore, then Oakland on the road, they'd won 15 of 17. And the knives were out.

"We're hoping Toronto will pull a Toronto," outfielder Darryl Hamilton confided.

"They are going to choke," pitcher Jaime Navarro predicted.

Choke? Winfield didn't seem to have any problems with swallowing as he became the first 40-year-old to drive in 100 runs: "I heard a lot about that stuff when I first came to Toronto. I don't want to hear it any more. This is a different bunch of guys now."

Very different: a multi-talented mix of homegrown kids, veteran mercenaries and emerging stars who knew they had to go out and get the job done through those nailbiting final five weeks of the season.

It wasn't easy. You could ask David Cone.

Coming over from the Mets in late August, the major league strikeout leader was seen as the final key to the championship, the man who would make the difference.

Too bad about his debut. Remember that sunny Saturday at the SkyDome when the Brewers ran wild? Eight steals, the most ever against Toronto, as Cone gave up seven earned runs in less than seven innings. His American League ERA was 9.45.

The next time was a little better: four earned runs in six innings against the Twins. The Jays scored 16, so it didn't matter.

After that, Cone could easily have gone 5-0 but the run support was pathetic. He beat Kansas City 1-0, lost 2-1 to Cleveland, beat Texas and New York 1-0 and 3-1, then lost 1-0 to Boston on Frank Viola's memorable one-hitter.

When the smoke had cleared, Cone was 4-3 as a Blue Jay. Yes, he had made a difference.

At the other end of the salary and publicity scale, so had Alfredo Griffin.

When shortstop Manuel Lee went down with a sore knee in late August, it seemed the Jays were in big trouble at a pivotal position. Could the 35-year-old Griffin, who'd looked shaky in the field and feeble at the plate in his rare appearances, adequately fill in?

Fill in? Playing with the same verve that earned him a share of AL rookie of the year honors in 1979, Alfredo played a

solid shortstop and turned the kind of double plays Lee had been missing.

At bat, he wasn't pretty. But somehow his bloops and bouncers found the holes, giving him a .270 average for September. In his last 10 starts before Lee returned on Oct. 2, Griff hit .371.

Yes, Alomar, Carter, Olerud, White, Borders and Lee had come through big-time all year. But when the collars got tight in September, where would this team have been without some steady old crocks named Griffin, Winfield, Maldonado and Morris? Hey, pass the Geritol.

It didn't look like Jack Morris needed any elixir on Sept. 17 at the SkyDome as he cruised toward becoming the Jays' first 20-game winner. Through seven innings, he'd only allowed the Cleveland Indians three hits and led 5-3. Just six more outs, and . . .

raaack! A two-run Albert Belle double in the eighth, and the game was tied. The Jays won it in extra innings, but Jack was outta there by then.

Six days later in Baltimore, Morris threw eight good innings, but Orioles rookie Arthur Rhodes threw eight great ones — beating the Jays 4-1.

When No. 20 finally came, on a dismal Sunday afternoon in Yankee Stadium, Jack had to wait for it.

Remember? That was the beginning of the last week of the season. The week when we *all* had to wait, and wait, and . . .

What was with those cursed Brewers? Couldn't they *ever* lose?

COLIN McCONNELL

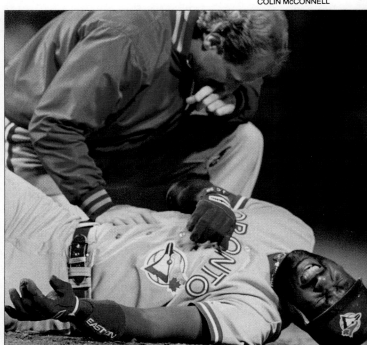

SPEAK TO ME, JOE, SPEAK TO ME. IT LOOKS SERIOUS, BUT ALL THAT PAIN CAME FROM A BALL FOULED OFF CARTER'S FOOT.

Since the all-star break, the Cheeseheads had posted the best record in the AL, going 46-27 to Oct. 1.

In September, the Jays played outstanding ball, winning 18 of 26. But the incredible Brewers were even better at 20-7.

Who were these guys?

Paul Molitor you know. For once, he didn't get hurt, but he inflicted plenty of damage on AL pitching with a .320 average.

Pat Listach you didn't know. The lithe shortstop wasn't even on the Brewers' opening day roster. But his .290 average, 93 runs and team-record 54 stolen bases made him a favorite for rookie of the year honors and played a huge role in the Brewers' success.

Throw in a back-from-the-dead Kevin Seitzer hitting .270 at third, a reborn Scotty Fletcher having a career year at second, outfielder Hamilton catching and stealing everything in sight while hitting .298 in right, future Hall of Famer Robin Yount doing his thing (and collecting his 3,000th hit) in centre, Greg Vaughn pounding 23 homers in left, and . . .

Wait. We haven't even mentioned the pitching. Can you believe 10 straight wins for *Chris Bosio*? And where did they come up with this rookie named Cal Eldred? He won 10 straight, too.

Mix in a little Navarro, Bill Wegman, Doug Henry and what have you got? The best team ERA in the league at 3.43, to go with the AL's second-best hitting at .268. (Toronto finished fifth in hitting at .263, and ninth in pitching at 3.91.)

The author of this amazing success story? Rookie manager Phil (Scrap Iron) Garner, who infected his boys with a pugnacious, never-say-die approach that carried them to an East Division record of 254 steals.

Could it also carry them to the championship?

On that rainy Sunday in Yankee Stadium, a lot of people thought it could. Milwaukee was just 2½ games back and rolling.

Remember that nerve-wracking day? The Jays scored nine runs in the first three innings off Scott Sanderson, and it appeared Jack's 20th was in the bag.

Then, in the top of the fifth, Danielle struck. Hurricane Danielle, that is, dealing a glancing blow to New York and bringing the game to a halt *before the fifth inning could be completed.*

Uh-oh. If the game was washed out, and Milwaukee beat Oakland . . .

An hour passed. Still pouring. Two hours. Could Morris come back after this long delay? Would the TV broadcast come back on if the game ever resumed?

Finally, as Star columnist Dave Perkins wrote: "Just when it was beginning to appear that God had become a Brewer fan, the rain stopped."

Morris threw another two innings to wrap up his 20th, and the Jays had their 92nd win — one more than they'd needed to outdistance the AL East by seven games in '91. (By the way, the TV broadcast never did come back. They stuck with a movie.)

Meanwhile, back in Milwaukee, the Brewers-A's game had also been delayed — by the crush of walk-up customers at the ticket windows. When they finally got going, nearly 55,000 fans saw a zany spectacle in which A's manager Tony La Russa announced himself as a pinch hitter and walked threateningly toward plate umpire Greg Kosc with bat in hand.

They also saw 333 pitches, three ejections and 13 walks in a four-hour marathon in which Milwaukee went 0 for 15 with runners in scoring position, and won again: 5-3. The beat goes on.

With two off-days, the Blue Jays had five games left, all at the SkyDome: two with last-place Boston, three with (uh-oh) the Tigers.

The Brewers, scheduled to play only West Division clubs down the stretch because they were the "swing" team, had six games: three in Seattle and three in Oakland.

The difference between Toronto and Milwaukee was 2½ games. The magic number was four.

After both teams took Monday off, the fun started Tuesday, Sept. 29, for the Jays with great news: Red Sox ace Roger Clemens had pulled a groin muscle and couldn't pitch. Projected starters for the series: Key vs. Danny Darwin and Cone vs. Matt Young.

Key, back to his old self for the stretch run after a rough July and August, did his job. Handed three runs in the first inning via hits from Devon White, Alomar, Winfield and Candy Maldonado, he cruised to a 5-2 win with late-inning help from Duane Ward and Tom Henke.

Then, for millions of fans in southern Ontario, it was time to tune in the radio for the play-by-play from Seattle. Eldred

MIKE SLAUGHTER

DON'T THEY WISH? MANUEL LEE HOLDS UP A YANKEE FAN'S SIGN FOR WINFIELD AS DEREK BELL LOOKS ON DURING SEPT. 27 APPEARANCE AT YANKEE STADIUM.

MIKE SLAUGHTER

RAINING ON JACK'S PARADE. MORRIS HAD TO ENDURE THIS TWO-HOUR RAIN DELAY BEFORE NOTCHING HIS 20TH AT YANKEE STADIUM.

was hot. Yount, Seitzer and Molitor rapped nine doubles. The Brewers won 7-4. The magic number was three.

The next night brought an unpleasant surprise. Boston manager Butch Hobson decided not to start the erratic Young, who was 0-for-the-season. Instead, the Jays would face Viola.

Cone pitched one of his finest games of the year, limiting Boston to four hits and one run. Viola pitched the game of his life.

Looking every bit the all-star he used to be, Mr. Sweet Music dominated the Jays so completely that many in the sellout crowd began thinking no-hitter early.

White burst that bubble with a clean single to lead off the ninth. But that was it, and the Jays were gone 1-0.

Back to the radio (and TV, as well, this night) for the inevitable Brewers victory. But then . . . a miracle!

The Brewers *LOST!*

Hey there, Ken Griffey, Tino Martinez and Bret Boone. Thanks for the homers, guys! Nice pitching, Tim Leary! Tim *Leary*? A 7-4 win for Seattle, and the magic number was two.

The next day, while the Jays were off, Seattle took on the Brewers again and led 2-0 after six innings. Could the Mariners do it again?

Nahhh! The Brewers win 7-2 in 10 innings, and the Jays' lead was down to two games.

Which brings us to the final weekend. The Jays have three with the Tigers; Milwaukee has three in Oakland against the West Division champs. The magic number is two.

At the SkyDome, it's the same matchup we saw that breezy April afternoon, oh so long ago, when the season began at Tiger Stadium: Morris vs. Bill Gullickson.

The result was Morris' league-leading 21st win, but it sure wasn't easy.

Leading 6-1 via homers by Alomar, Maldonado and Pat Borders after two, Cactus Jack was less than overpowering, leaving with an 8-6 lead after six.

After Mark Eichhorn served up Mickey Tettleton's 32nd homer, the bullpen phone was ringing and it was another one-run nailbiter.

But Ward and Henke blew 'em away in the eighth and ninth, and the Jays were on the verge of their third divisional championship in four years. They could become the first team since the 1980-81 Yankees to win back-to-back titles if only Oakland could . . .

Nahhh! The Brewers win 3-2 in extra innings.

Still, even if Milwaukee had won the final two games and Toronto lost both, the Jays were assured of a tie. The playoff game (God forbid!) would be at the SkyDome on Monday.

Now it's Saturday, Oct. 3, Winfield's 41st birthday. Beautiful blue skies over the SkyDome, 21C and . . . the roof closed, of course.

47

JEFF GOODE

THE FINAL OUT. DUANE WARD GETS READY TO CELEBRATE AFTER
JOHN OLERUD CATCHES POP-UP IN TITLE-CLINCHING GAME.

CELEBRATION TIME FOR ALFREDO GRIFFIN AND
DAVE WINFIELD AFTER GAME THAT WON THE EAST.

Inside, the 61st sellout crowd in 80 dates could smell victory in the air.

The magic number was Juan.

What a performance! Juan Guzman, struggling all through September to regain his touch after missing three weeks with shoulder problems, struck out seven of the first 12 Tigers he faced and allowed only one hit through eight innings.

Joe Carter, who'd driven in the winner against California when the Jays clinched in '91, gave Guzman all the support he needed with a towering two-run shot over the centre-field fence in the first inning. It was his 34th homer and 119th RBI.

Fittingly, Big Dave drove in the Jays' third run two innings later and was serenaded by the world's largest "Happy Birthday" chorus.

When Cito Gaston turned the ball over to Henke with a 3-0 lead in the ninth, it seemed the celebrations could begin. Henke hadn't blown a save since July 24.

But 96 wins didn't come easily to this team. Why should the clincher be different?

Henke looked nervous, even shaky. After getting Lou Whitaker, he surrendered singles to Travis Fryman and Cecil Fielder. Then a walk to Tettleton. Bases loaded, tying run on first. Dangerous Rob Deer, with 32 homers in only 388 at-bats, at the plate.

Whew! Got him on a pop-up. Two out.

Then a walk to Scott Livingstone. The shutout was gone, 3-1, and here comes Cito.

In from the bullpen comes Mr. Intensity, Duane Ward, to pitch to Dan Gladden.

Wooosh. Wooosh. Pop-up!

Olerud's got it!

Milwaukee is dead.

The shadows have vanished.

Now, *bring on the A's!*

DICK LOEK

48

SHOWER TIME.
HAPPY-GO-LUCKY DEREK
BELL GETS DRENCHED
WITH CHAMPAGNE.
TURNER WARD IS THE
POURER.

HUG FROM THE BOSS.
JUAN GUZMAN, WHO
SPUN A ONE-HITTER IN
CLINCHING GAME, GETS
A THANK YOU FROM
CITO GASTON.

JEFF GOODE

MIKE SLAUGHTER

BY DAVE PERKINS

MVP

Robbie Alomar finds more ways to beat you than any other player in baseball

There still are a handful of people around who will tell you that Charlie Gehringer, the famed Mechanical Man of the Detroit Tigers, made this play at second base.

He fielded a ground ball that had passed between first baseman Rudy York and the foul line.

Think about that: A routine double by today's standards, a triple if the ball is hit well. But Gehringer got to the ball and, so the stories go, got to it in time to throw the batter out at first base.

There are witnesses around who will testify that Gehringer did this half a century ago. He did it four times, apparently, although once should be enough to construct the legend.

The story about Gehringer is mentioned to Roberto Alomar and he takes time to digest it. (He is a rarity for a baseball player in that he sometimes stops and thinks about what is being said to him.)

"Ground ball down the line, first baseman can't reach it?" Alomar asks. "But the second baseman can?"

He ponders briefly, painting the mental picture.

"No, I don't think I could do that one," he finally says.

Somewhere, a large bell rings all by itself. Birds stop flying. Fish stop swimming.

So there is — after all the evidence to the contrary for the past two years — something Roberto Alomar cannot do on a baseball field.

An entire city has been walking around believing that Alomar changes his clothes in phone booths, that he can do anything and everything out there between the lines.

Mostly because he has, of course.

The Blue Jays have never had a player who could win a game in more ways than Roberto Alomar.

If he is not already the best player in the history of the franchise, then he will be when he's older and more experienced.

Sure, just wait until he's a ripe old 25.

Some mature types like to believe that youth is wasted on the young, but there's nothing wasted on this guy, at least in the baseball sense. He's 24, plays the game like 34.

He's a kid at heart with a veteran's knowledge and understanding of the game.

If he wasn't born with great baseball instincts — his father, Sandy Alomar, was a 15-year big league veteran — then he sure was raised with them.

Some things he does on the field simply cannot be taught.

Ask Kevin McReynolds, the lumbering outfielder for the Kansas City Royals.

If there needed to be one defensive play to stand out above all other in the Blue Jays' pennant-winning season, it's easy to guess which one would get McReynolds' nomination.

On Sept. 9 in Royals Stadium, the Jays led 1-0 in the second inning, McReynolds on second base and two out.

Brian McRae looped a little line drive directly back over the pitcher's head. With two out, here came McReynolds turning third with the tying run.

Except here came Alomar from second base, reaching to spear the ball on the hop before it bounced into centre field. He got there on the Royals Stadium AstroTurf and gloved the ball, thereby saving the tying run.

All but two of three big league second basemen — good players, all — would have been satisfied with the play so far, with merely getting there and saving the run.

Not Alomar. Without even breaking stride, running toward left-centre field, he wheeled and fired a strike to third base. Just in case McReynolds was slow in returning to the bag, or in case he was wandering.

He was wandering. He was three feet from third base. The throw nailed him completely. End of the inning. End of the game, really. The Royals never got another man past the scene of this crime and the Jays made that run stand up for a 1-0 win.

What a play!

That's usually what someone ends up saying when Alo-

TAKING THE HIGH ROAD, ALOMAR SOARS OVER BREWERS' KEVIN SEITZER TO COMPLETE YET ANOTHER DOUBLE PLAY.

mar's around.

If he couldn't hit his weight — even in kilos — and couldn't steal 50-plus bases, he would still be an asset to a winning team.

That he spent the entire season in the thick of the American League's top 10 batting race, that he drove in more than 70 runs and scored more than 100 and drew a career-high total of walks and seemed to spend more time on base than some teams, only makes him the complete baseball player.

That's "complete" as in, if the Blue Jays didn't have him, they'd be completely cooked.

There shouldn't be a Blue Jay fan out there who doesn't agree.

Dave Winfield showed up this season and performed like a youngster, far outperforming anyone's wildest expectations. Joe Carter was Joe Carter, driving in a ton of runs and hitting homers and showing up for roll call every day. John Olerud made some progress toward his ultimate potential and Candy Maldonado hit well and the bottom of the order chipped in with some numbers.

But take away Alomar and the hole would have been too big to fill.

The radio talk shows in this town reveal Blue Jay fans to be the most demanding in baseball. Never satisfied.

Where else could you find callers, after a victory, complain-

ing because the game was too close? In this town, they wanted the manager fired if the win wasn't lopsided.

But has anyone ever wasted his or her time moaning about Alomar? Has anyone ever complained about the way he plays ball?

Fans like to whine about players' salaries, but you never hear Alomar included on the list of those who make far too much. He signed a four-year contract extension last winter for $18.5 million and think hard: Have you ever heard anyone yet suggest it wasn't money well spent?

Of course, if everyone played ball the way Alomar did, no one would ever complain about salaries.

Remember the 22-2 game? Remember the way the Blue Jays were humiliated by the Brewers that wacky night?

Most of the Jays players laughed it off, the way you are supposed to with blowout defeats.

But this was worse than a blowout. It was a team-wide embarrassment.

Alomar was the only Blue Jay who showed it.

In the ninth inning, he dived for a ground ball for the second out. Then he dived for a ground ball trying to get the third out. His body language told the world he had had enough of this disgrace.

Afterward, body language was the only thing on which he could be quoted. He was angry and it was good to see; no one

TONY BOCK

'AIR ALOMAR' STEALS THIRD BASE AGAINST CLEVELAND. HE LED THE TEAM IN BOTH STOLEN BASES AND BATTING FOR THE SECOND YEAR.

else took it nearly this hard.

A couple of times, Alomar has let it be known he didn't like the way things went down on this ball club.

He is not a soapbox kind of guy, not a preacher. He would rather play by example than make a speech.

He is one of the few ball players who understands the function of the press, for instance, how it can be used to get across a particular point.

This was the source of the great staring situation.

Alomar felt that Gene Tenace, the team's bench coach and someone with whom Alomar does not always see eye to eye, was glaring at him critically for a first-inning sacrifice bunt.

Now, a first-inning sacrifice bunt, especially with the lead-off man already at second base, is usually a waste of a valuable out and, therefore, a bad move.

There are times, though, it might make sense and this time, in Texas in early September, it did. It did to Alomar, anyway, and since he had the bat in his hands at the time, that is all that matters.

He bunted and Joe Carter promptly drove in the run from third base with a sacrifice fly. Alomar, though, felt Tenace had been unspokenly disapproving.

He sought out a reporter and suggested, somewhat cryptically, that someone was giving him the evil eye. He didn't name names.

The story hung in the air for two days like a bad smell. Alomar clammed up, at least publicly. He huddled with Cito Gaston, said his bit privately and cleared the air.

Whether he handled it rightly or wrongly, he got it off his chest, at least, and got back to the business of playing baseball.

He may have done this business better than anyone else in the American League this year.

Guessing the voting for most valuable player is always dangerous, especially on a team like the Blue Jays, who have more than one candidate.

Alomar would be no less thrilled by an MVP award than would any other deserving big leaguer, but — and you have to believe him on this — he didn't want to win that individual award a fraction as much as he wanted the Blue Jays to get to, and win, the World Series.

"I had some dreams when I was a boy," Alomar says. "I dreamed to play in the big leagues and I've done that. I dreamed to play with my brother and we've done that. I dreamed to be an all-star and I've done that and I dreamed to win the World Series."

An MVP would be the ultimate personal addition to that list and would maybe leave the Gehringer play as the one and only thing he hasn't done on a baseball field. And don't bet against that, either.

KEN FAUGHT

PATTI GOWER

NO. 1 WITH FANS, ALOMAR IS ALSO ONE OF THE MOST ACCOMMODATING JAYS, EVEN AT SPRING TRAINING.

GETTING THE KINKS OUT BEFORE TAKING THE PLATE. ROBBIE WAS THE ONLY JAY REGULAR TO TOP .300 MARK.

SHOW TIME

On paper, it was the Jays in five, six at the most. Even Vegas rated them a confident 3-to-2 favorite to knock off the A's.

But then, the odds were a trillion to one against the Braves and Twins meeting for last year's World Series after both had finished last in 1990.

And the American League Championship Series isn't played on paper — though the stuff that carpets the Sky-Dome comes pretty close, chemically speaking. Moreover, after 162 games, the Jays and A's had finished with identical records: 96 wins and 66 losses. Oakland had a much easier time winning what had been considered the AL's tougher division — until the Milwaukee Brewers headed west this fall.

The Jays and A's had gone 6-6 in games against each other, each team winning three at home and three on the road. That's what most people, and Oxford, call even.

So, where was the Jays' big edge? Starting pitching, for starters. The announced matchups were: Jack Morris (21-6, 4.04 ERA) against Dave Stewart (12-10, 3.66); David Cone (4-3, 2.55) against Mike Moore (17-12, 3.66); and Juan Guzman (16-5, 2.64) against Ron Darling (15-10, 3.66). With the Mets before he was traded, Cone was 13-7 with a 2.88 ERA and 214 strikeouts (tops in the majors).

That gave the Jays an ERA edge of about half a run a game, a 10-win bulge and 11 fewer losses among the starters alone. In fact, none of Oakland's starters, if we get back to paper again, could have made the Jays' starting three not even Stewart, who was 5-0 in league championship play.

The Jays' edge was almost as commanding 60 feet, 6 inches away. Toronto had outscored the A's 780-745 and outhomered them 163-142. The Jays also had an RBI edge of 44 over their west coast rivals. Moreover, the A's had made 32 more errors than the Jays did, and they didn't have an outfielder who could carry Devon White's shoes to the park, or an infielder in the same galaxy as Robbie Alomar.

Only in stolen bases, even with Rickey Henderson frequently on the shelf, did Oakland have an offensive edge, 143 to 129. But no one was forgetting how Henderson had run the Jays rightout of the '89 playoffs.

This year, however, Rickey, slowed by maladies of both head and foot, had stolen one base fewer than Alomar. But no one doubted that, come the playoffs, he would again turn on the jets. In fact, boss Pat Gillick said the key for the Jays would be keeping Rickey off the bases.

It was also worth noting that the A's were all finished with the Jays before Toronto acquired Cone and before Oakland traded away Jose Canseco — still the most devastating hitter in baseball when in the mood. Instead of Canseco, the A's had Ruben Sierra (17 homers and 87 RBIs).

One of two areas where most observers gave the A's an edge was in managing, although Cito Gaston had the next-best record to Tony La Russa's since the Jays skipper was promoted from batting coach. This year, however, had been La Russa's finest, winning from a dugout that resembled a hospital emergency ward with a team that wasn't supposed to make it even if it had stayed healthy.

The Jays, on the other hand, had been everyone's favorite to repeat in the East, and Gaston was under attack most of the year even though his team clung to the lead almost every inch of the way. Fans who called radio talk shows made him and Kelly Gruber their targets. The hosts, paid to produce controversy, poured gasoline on every complaint that dribbled in.

Oakland's other apparent edge was the Eck. Dennis Eckersley was as good as he had ever been in '92, the premier reliever in baseball (7-1, 51 saves, 1.91 ERA). Even the Jays' Tom Henke and Duane Ward, with 46 saves between them, weren't in his neighborhood.

The A's also had Mark McGwire going for them. Messed up by a batting coach last year, he had regained his old form and would have led the league in homers if he hadn't joined Oakland's walking wounded for almost a month late in the season. As it was, he hit 42 homers (just one less than Juan Gonzalez of the Rangers) and drove in 104 runs. But both Joe Carter (119 RBIs) and Dave Winfield (108) had topped the giant first baseman in delivering runners, and Oakland didn't have another player with even 90 RBIs.

But the Jays never made anything easy, and they went into

DICK LOEK

ONE BIG QUESTION: COULD CITO GASTON MATCH WITS WITH TONY LA RUSSA?

the playoffs with a little bit of self-constructed controversy. General manager Gillick told a talk show host that he figured Jimmy Key, winner of his last five games but sporting a 13-13 record and 3.53 ERA, should be the No. 3 starter.

That was before Juan Guzman went out and clinched the East for them in the second-last game of the season, with a sparkling one-hitter against the Tigers. Detroit manager Sparky Anderson was so impressed he called Guzman the best pitcher in the AL, when healthy.

Could Guzman and his 16-5 record watch the playoffs from the bullpen, just because it took him a few games to regain his form after returning from the DL?

With the Jays, such a thing was all too possible. Fans recalled how the club had decided not to give Guzman a second start in the '91 playoffs — in which he was their only winner — and wondered if they might shoot themselves in the radar gun again. Fortunately, sanity prevailed, even if belatedly so.

One other edge the Jays had was that it was their turn to host the first two games, and they were 53-28 at home.

A TRICK ENDING FOR JACK MORRIS

GAME 1

A's 4 at Jays 3

Jack took the loss and Cito took the blame.

That, in a catcher's mitt, was the story of Game 1 of the American League Championship Series, played before a sometimes silent and sometimes hysterical crowd of 51,039 at the SkyDome.

A fine game, it unfolded like a Jack Morris play we had all seen before — except this one had a trick ending.

You remember the script. There was Jack, giving up back-to-back homers to big banger Mark McGwire and catcher Terry Steinbach in the second inning to go down three runs. Not to worry. We all knew what Jack would do — grind it out, become stingier than Scrooge, hold the A's in check until his teammates had a chance to catch up.

That's just what the Jays' $15 million man did. He shut the A's down on a single hit for six innings, from the third through the eighth. Meanwhile, Dave Winfield and Pat Borders blast-ed homers of their own, and John Olerud socked a clutch single with Winfield on second to tie the score in the bottom of the eighth.

That's when the crowd, sullenly silent in the second, almost tore the roof off the dome. Cito Gaston, appearing sphinx-like as usual in the dugout, was all of a sudden looking mighty good. Forget that he hadn't sent any runners. Even a conservative Jays team should be able to take these guys now. Ol' Mo, as in momentum, was on their side.

But not for long. Cito decided to let Morris come back to the mound to pitch the ninth, and to face lefthanded batter Harold Baines, the gimpy DH who all season long had appeared to be headed toward early retirement at age 33.

Two pitches later, Baines launched a rocket to right, off the second deck. Game over and everybody knew it.

Sure, the Jays had come back in the ninth all season long, but this time they would be facing Dennis Eckersley, the best reliever in baseball.

Moreover, the Eck would be facing the bottom of the Jays order. He had his serious game face on, but he must have been laughing himself silly inside. Even manager Tony La Russa stopped pacing.

To their credit, the Jays managed to scratch out a single, by

COLIN McCONNELL

THIS FAN HAD EVERYTHING EXCEPT A WIN BY THE BLUE JAYS IN GAME 1.

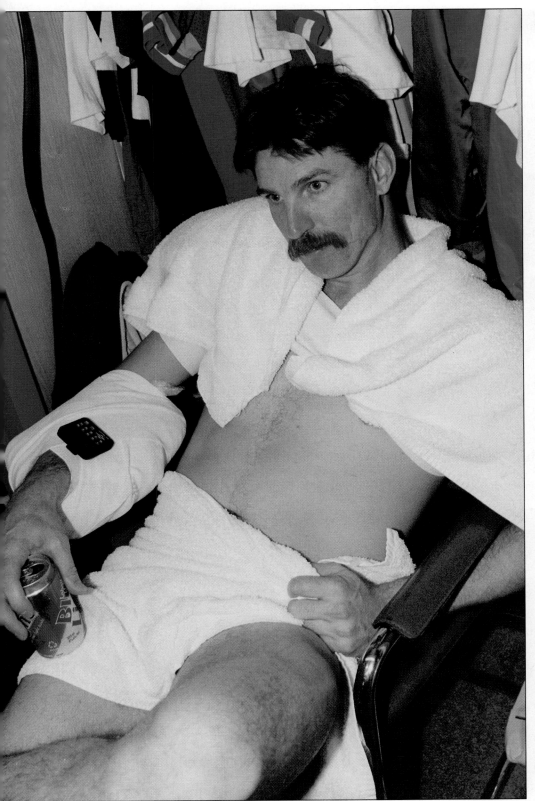

RON BULL

'WHY DIDN'T I THROW BAINES A FASTBALL?' MORRIS ASKS HIMSELF.

Oops!

ATHLETICS 4 at BLUE JAYS 3

Oakland	ab	r	h	bi	bb	so	avg.
RHenderson lf	2	0	0	0	2	0	.000
Lansford 3b	4	0	0	0	0	0	.000
Sierra rf	4	0	0	0	0	0	.000
Baines dh	4	2	3	1	0	0	.750
McGwire 1b	3	1	1	2	1	1	.333
Steinbach c	4	1	1	1	0	0	.250
WWilson cf	4	0	1	0	0	1	.250
Bordick ss	4	0	0	0	0	1	.000
Blankenship 2b	2	0	0	0	1	1	.000
Totals	**31**	**4**	**6**	**4**	**4**	**4**	

Toronto	ab	r	h	bi	bb	so	avg.
White cf	3	0	1	0	2	0	.333
RAlomar 2b	4	0	1	0	0	0	.250
Carter rf–1b	4	0	1	0	0	0	.250
Winfield dh	4	2	2	1	0	0	.500
Olerud 1b	3	0	1	1	1	0	.333
1-DBell pr–rf	0	0	0	0	0	0	—
Maldonado lf	4	0	0	0	0	2	.000
Gruber 3b	4	0	0	0	0	0	.000
Borders c	4	1	1	1	0	0	.250
Lee ss	3	0	1	0	0	0	.333
a-Sprague ph	1	0	1	0	0	0	1.000
2-Griffin pr	0	0	0	0	0	0	—
Totals	**34**	**3**	**9**	**3**	**3**	**2**	

Oakland	030 000 001	— 4	6 1
Toronto	000 011 010	— 3	9 0

a-singled for Lee in the 9th.

1-ran for Olerud in the 8th. 2-ran for Sprague in the 9th.

E—RHenderson (1). LOB—Oakland 4, Toronto 7. 2B—Winfield (1). HR—Winfield (1) off Stewart, Borders (1) off Stewart, Baines (1) off JaMorris, McGwire (1) off JaMorris, Steinbach (1) off JaMorris. RBIs—Baines (1), McGwire 2 (2), Steinbach (1), Winfield (1), Olerud (1), Borders (1). SB—WWilson (1), RAlomar (1). GIDP—Lansford, Steinbach, RAlomar, Gruber.

Runners left in scoring position—Oakland 3 (Sierra, WWilson, Bordick); Toronto 3 (RAlomar, Carter 2).

DP—Oakland 2 (Bordick, Blankenship and McGwire), (Bordick, Blankenship and McGwire); Toronto 2 (JaMorris, Lee and Olerud), (Lee, RAlomar and Olerud).

Oakland	ip	h	r	er	bb	so	np	era
Stewart	7 ⅔	7	3	3	3	2	110	3.52
JeRussell W, 1–0	⅓	1	0	0	0	0	12	0.00
Eckersley S, 1	1	1	0	0	0	1	13	0.00

Toronto	ip	h	r	er	bb	so	np	era
JaMorris L, 0–1	9	6	4	4	4	4	121	4.00

Inherited runners-scored—JeRussell 1–1. WP—JaMorris. Umpires—Home, Denkinger; First, Young; Second, Clark; Third, Merrill; Left, Brinkman; Right, Coble. T–2:47. A–51,039.

How the runs scored

Athletics' second: Morris pitching. Baines led off with a single to centre. McGwire drilled a 1-0 pitch to left-centre for a home run, scoring Baines as well. Steinbach lined an 0-2 pitch to left for a home run. Wilson struck out. Bordick struck out. Blankenship struck out. **Athletics 3, Blue Jays 0.**

Jays' fifth: Stewart pitching. Gruber popped out to second. Borders drove the first pitch to left for a home run. Lee lined out to centre. White singled to left and took second on Henderson's fielding error. Alomar lined out to second. **Athletics 3, Blue Jays 1.**

Jays' sixth: Carter grounded out, pitcher to first. Winfield slammed a 2-1 pitch to left-centre for a home run. Olerud flew out to left. Maldonado struck out. **Athletics 3, Blue Jays 2.**

Jays' eighth: Alomar grounded out short to first. Carter popped out to short. Winfield doubled to right-centre. Russell replaced Stewart. Olerud singled to centre, driving in Winfield. Maldonado hit into a fielder's choice, third to second. **Athletics 3, Blue Jays 3.**

Athletics' ninth: Leading off, Baines drilled a 1-0 pitch to right for a home run. McGwire grounded out, third to first. Steinbach flew out to right. Wilson beat out an infield single to short. With Bordick up, Wilson stole second. Bordick flew out to right. **Athletics 4, Blue Jays 3.**

pinch hitter Ed Sprague. But Eckersley disposed of Kelly Gruber, Borders and Devon White without working up a sweat, getting all three to hit weakly to shortstop Mike Bordick.

Even fans who, minutes before, had nodded sagely when Morris trudged back to the mound were ready to form lynch mobs. Within seconds, they had forgotten all about the Morris who had set the Braves down without a run for 10 innings during that classic final game of the 1991 World Series.

But, of course, it wasn't Jack they wanted to lynch; it was Cito.

COLIN McCONNELL

Didn't he know Jack usually gave up four runs a game?

Didn't he know Duane Ward was almost untouchable this season?

Wasn't lefty Jimmy Key seen warming up in the bullpen, ready to fan Baines or knock him out of the game in favor of a pinch hitter. On sports talk shows following the game, it was two to one in favor of lynching.

Cito was unrepentant. "I figure Jack's pitched well enough this year to give him a shot to go out and win the game," he said. But there had been lingering doubts right from the season opener about who decides when it's time for Morris to give up the ball — Cito or Jack?

"I felt I did the best I could," Morris said. "They beat me fair and square. I'm not going to hang my head.

"I'm not quitting," he added. "All it means is that we have to win four out of six instead of four out of seven."

No one could say Gaston was outmanaged by the A's skipper in this thriller. La Russa's one big move was bringing in Jeff Russell to pitch to Olerud, after Dave Winfield had doubled off starter Dave Stewart. Olerud fought off two unhittable pitches, then drilled a single up the middle to score Winfield and tie the game.

Russell, who was brought in just to get Olerud and failed miserably, still earned the win thanks to Baines' blast.

Stewart, who had a so-so 12-10 record during the season, pitched like the Stewart of old, the one who is 5-0 in AL playoff games. "A lot of oddsmakers go broke," he noted, referring to the fact that his team was made a 3-to-2 underdog by Las Vegas betting parlors.

The whole game, except for the dingers, was well pitched and well played, with Gruber, Joe Carter and Ruben Sierra making sparkling grabs in the field.

Jays fans couldn't take much joy from the fact that their heroes had out-hit the A's 9-6.

But they could take some heart from the way the Jays fought back from the early 3-0 deficit. This team wasn't like the Jays of old — and there were six games left to prove it.

BIG ADIOS! MARK McGWIRE DRILLS MORRIS MISTAKE FOR A TWO-RUN HOMER.

GOLD GLOVE GRAB. KELLY GRUBER SHOWS HE'S STILL GREAT IN THE FIELD IF NOT AT THE PLATE.

MIKE SLAUGHTER

THE HIRED GUN IS RIGHT ON TARGET

GAME 2

A's 1 at Jays 3

Okay, here's what you do:

Make a fist. Now, push it into the pit of your stomach — hard. Now, give it a twist.

Now you know how millions of Blue Jays fans felt at 11.20 p.m., Oct. 8, 1992.

We had knots in our stomachs, fear in our hearts, even prayers on our lips.

The cause of all this distress? Mark McGwire of the Oakland A's, coiled like a knock-kneed cobra at home plate in the ninth inning, awaiting his first pitch from Jays reliever Tom Henke.

Remember? The score is 3-1 Jays. Eric Fox is dancing off first, running for Harold Baines. McGwire, who had homered in Game 1, represents the tying run.

Some of us in the leather-lunged mob of 51,114 at the Sky-Dome are pressing fingernails painfully into palms. Some

watching at home have averted eyes from TV screens. A few radio listeners, unable to bear the tension, have switched stations "just for a minute."

Now, here comes the pitch. McGwire SWINGS! *It's a long belt to left! Looks like it's got the distance! That ball is going, going. . .*

But first, a look at what brought us to this gut-wrenching situation.

After losing the opener at home, this is a must-win game for Toronto. To limp off to Oakland down two games to none would be too horrible to contemplate. Already, some fair-weather fans are using the C word.

Not that there was any lack of enthusiasm at the flag-festooned dome. The cheers began as country and western star George Fox sang "O Canada," swelled when Olympic heroes Marnie McBean and Mark McKoy threw out ceremonial first pitches, and reached mega-decibels when David Cone whiffed Rickey Henderson on three pitches to start the game.

Yes, Mr. Cone would give us plenty to cheer about this warm Thursday night.

With his shark eyes, thin lips and pallid cheeks, the 29-year-old ex-Met looked like a Las Vegas blackjack dealer. He was dealing a wicked mix of fastballs, sliders and split-fingered bullets that had the A's flummoxed.

But A's starter Mike Moore was having a fine night, too. After four scoreless innings, each team had only managed one hit.

RICHARD LAUTENS

DALE BRAZAO

FAN CROSSES HER FINGERS AS CONE FACES SLUGGER MARK McGWIRE.

COOL AS A RIVERBOAT GAMBLER, DAVID CONE DEALS ANOTHER FASTBALL.

59

CONEHEADS DAVID WELLS AND MIKE TIMLIN GET INTO GAME FROM BULLPEN.

RON BULL

It was a typical Cone game. In his previous five starts, the Jays had scored a total of six runs for him. But he's tough, this kid from Kansas. And tonight, he has more than a little help from his friends.

Top of the fifth. Willie Wilson on second, Mike Bordick on first with one out. Walt Weiss at the plate. Cone gets the sign from Borders. The pitch . . .

The runners are breaking for second and third. Double steal! Cone's pitch is off Borders' left shin pad. As Borders chases the ball toward the Jays dugout, Wilson is turning for home. He scores!

But wait. Cito is gesturing to home plate umpire Larry Young. Wilson is being summoned from the dugout and placed at third, all because of a play Borders *did not* make.

The ball had rolled into the dugout, deliberately untouched by Borders, so the ruling was that Wilson and Bordick were entitled to only one base. The A's were still off the scoreboard, and they stayed off as Cone fanned Weiss and Rickey.

Now it's the bottom of the fifth, Candy Maldonado on first. Moore's first pitch to Kelly Gruber is a fastball inside.

WHAM! Gruber, hitless in the series and the hecklers' favorite target, lined the ball 383 feet over the left-field wall. The obligatory fireworks explode, but you can't hear them for the crowd.

Two innings later, Gruber expands his heroics by doubling, advancing on a Borders grounder and scoring on Manuel Lee's sacrifice fly. Can the A's retaliate against Cone?

They have a dandy chance in the eighth, when Weiss singles and steals second. Now Rickey lifts a high fly to the warning track in left. Maldonado makes the catch. Weiss tags and streaks for third.

Here comes Maldonado's throw — a perfect one-hopper to Gruber. Weiss s-l-i-d-e-s . . . OUT!

Now, the nervous ninth. Cone has thrown 100 pitches, but tells Cito he's okay. Leading off is Ruben Sierra, the sweet-swinging Puerto Rican who's supposed to make Oakland forget Jose Canseco.

Uh-oh! There's a shot to the wall in left-centre. By the time Devon White corrals it, Sierra is on third.

Harold Baines, whose ninth-inning homer had killed the Jays the night before, is up. Ball one from Cone. Ball two. Cone is clearly out of gas. Here comes Cito.

And here comes Henke, who'd faltered so badly against Detroit in the pennant clincher five days earlier. *What about Ward?* Forget it. You know Cito.

Ball three to Baines. Then a strike, and . . . base hit! Sierra scores.

Which is where you came in, isn't it? McGwire SWINGS! *That ball is going, going, going.* . . *FOUL!* By 15 feet.

Two pitches later, McGwire lifts a routine fly to right. Terry Steinbach strikes out. Wilson forces Fox.

Thanks, Tom. Never doubted you for a moment, buddy. All tied up now. On to Oakland!

GRUBER BLASTS TWO-RUN HOMER IN FIFTH TO WIN THE GAME.

RON BULL

In flight!

ATHLETICS 1 at BLUE JAYS 3
Game Two

Oakland	ab	r	h	bi	bb	so	avg.
RHenderson lf	4	0	0	0	0	2	.000
Lansford 3b	4	0	0	0	0	1	.000
Sierra rf	3	1	1	0	1	0	.143
Baines dh	4	0	2	1	0	0	.625
1–Fox pr	0	0	0	0	0	0	—
McGwire 1b	4	0	0	0	0	1	.143
Steinbach c	4	0	1	0	0	3	.250
WWilson cf	4	0	1	0	0	0	.250
Bordick 2b	2	0	0	0	1	0	.000
Weiss ss	2	0	1	0	1	1	.500
Totals	31	1	6	1	3	7	

Toronto	ab	r	h	bi	bb	so	avg.
White cf	3	0	0	0	1	2	.167
RAlomar 2b	3	0	1	0	1	0	.286
Carter rf	3	0	0	0	1	1	.143
Winfield dh	3	0	0	0	1	0	.286
Olerud 1b	3	0	0	0	0	0	.167
Maldonado lf	2	1	0	0	1	0	.000
Gruber 3b	3	2	2	2	0	0	.286
Borders c	3	0	1	0	0	0	.286
Lee ss	2	0	0	1	0	0	.200
Totals	25	3	4	3	5	3	

Oakland	000 000 001	—1	6 0
Toronto	000 020 10x	—3	4 0

1–ran for Baines in the 9th.

LOB—Oakland 6, Toronto 4. 2B—WWilson (1), Gruber (1). 3B—Sierra (1). HR—Gruber (1) off Moore. RBIs—Baines (2), Gruber 2 (2), Lee (1). SB—WWilson 3 (4), Bordick (1), Weiss 2 (2), RAlomar (2), Carter (1). CS—Sierra (1), White (1). SF—Lee. GIDP—Carter.

Runners left in scoring position—Oakland 4 (RHenderson 2, Lansford 2); Toronto 2 (Winfield, Maldonado).

Runners moved up—Olerud, Borders.

DP—Oakland 1 (Lansford, Bordick and McGwire); Toronto 1 (Maldonado and Gruber).

Oakland	ip	h	r	er	bb	so	np	era
Moore L, 0–1	7	4	3	3	4	3	105	3.86
Corsi	⅔	0	0	0	1	0	7	0.00
Parrett	⅓	0	0	0	0	0	4	0.00

Toronto	ip	h	r	er	bb	so	np	era
Cone W, 1–0	8	5	1	1	3	6	109	1.12
Henke S, 1	1	1	0	0	1	1	12	0.00

Cone pitched to 1 batter in the 9th. Umpires—Home, Young; First, Clark; Second, Merrill; Third, Brinkman; Left, Coble; Right, Denkinger. T—2:58. A—51,114.

How the runs scored

Jays' fifth: Moore pitching. Olerud lined out to centre. Maldonado drew a walk. Gruber lined the first pitch in to the Jays' bullpen in left for a home run, scoring Maldonado as well. Borders singled to centre. Lee lined out to centre. White lined out to short. **Blue Jays 2, Athletics 0.**

Jays' seventh: Gruber led off by pulling a double down the left-field line. Borders grounded out pitcher to second to first, advancing Gruber to third. Lee's sacrifice fly to left scored Gruber. White struck out. **Blue Jays 3, Athletics 0.**

Athletics' ninth: Cone pitching. Sierra led off with a triple to left-centre. With a 2-0 count on Baines, Henke replaced Cone. Baines singled through the middle, scoring Sierra. Fox ran for Baines. McGwire flew out to right. Steinbach struck out. Wilson grounded into a fielder's choice, short to second. **Blue Jays 3, Athletics 1.**

JUAN AND ONLY ONE DOES IT AGAIN

GAME 3

Jays 7 at A's 5

All season long, the Jays had shown they were never going to do things the easy way. And, in Game 3 of the playoffs at Oakland Coliseum, they didn't.

But they did hang on for a 7-5 win in an erratic tussle, in which the Athletics made three errors and allowed the winning run to score on a wild pitch.

West coast sportswriters warned eastern scribes long before the first pitch that balls would probably be flying around like pigeons at a picnic in this contest, mostly because they always do during day games at the Coliseum. They were right.

However, several of the Jays' key hits were launched from unlikely sources. Manuel Lee, who went to spring training fighting for his job, drove in two with a triple and scored another. Candy Maldonado hit the first post-season home run of his career and drove in two.

The Athletics didn't get to see Jays starter Juan Guzman at his best, but they had seen enough of him by the time manager Cito Gaston dispatched him to the showers between the sixth and seventh innings. He departed with a 3-2 lead, which sounds a lot better than it looked.

For Toronto fans, biting their nails back home, this wasn't the Juan and only Juan they were expecting. That Juan, 16-5 on the season with a sparkling 2.64 ERA, usually had a nightmarish inning early, then blew the opposition away until Duane Ward and Tom Henke showed up to throw him a life preserver, whether it was needed or not.

Juan endured several nightmares in Game 3. In the fourth, Ruben Sierra doubled and was driven in by hot-hitting Harold Baines. Up came Mark McGwire, whom Guzman had the good sense to hit before the giant slugger hit him.

But catcher Terry Steinbach drove in Baines with a single, and it looked like curtains for Guzman when Mike Bordick lined out to Joe Carter, with McGwire on third. A high hard throw from Carter nailed McGwire, however, with catcher Pat Borders sticking it to the Oakland giant, who charged the plate like Lawrence Taylor going after a quarterback's head.

Then, still leading 3-2 in the sixth, Guzman was in trouble again after easily retiring big guns Baines and McGwire to start the inning. Before Cito could get to the bullpen phone, the bases were loaded. Shortstop Walter Weiss, pitiful at the plate in the series, grounded to John Olerud and Guzman was out of the inning — and the game — but not out of trouble.

Ward, normally the most reliable reliever on the staff (1.95 ERA), brought a can of gasoline with him instead of a fire hose when he arrived to pitch the seventh. He gave up two runs in his inning of work.

There was some tragic managing — but not by Cito. Oakland skipper Tony La Russa is everyone's favorite for AL manager of the year, but this time just about every move backfired.

When the Athletics closed to 5-4 against Ward in the seventh, La Russa sent in righthander Jim Corsi to start the eighth. He retired Roberto Alomar easily, but was quickly replaced by another righty, Jeff Russell, who gave up a walk and a single and allowed Winfield to score the eventual winner on a wild pitch.

Meanwhile, La Russa inserted the usually surehanded Lance Blankenship at second in the seventh inning and he promptly made two errors. Blankenship was there because La Russa pinch hit for Bordick, the regular second baseman and club leader in batting average during the season, because he was having a terrible series.

Even Dennis Eckersley made La Russa look bad. Although the Eck usually appears only in save situations, the Oakland manager called for him in the top of the ninth to keep his team within a run of the Jays, who were clinging to a 6-5 lead. It looked easy, with two out and Lee still sitting at first after an inning-opening walk.

But Carter, whom Eckersley usually owns, singled Lee to third. The shortstop scored the insurance run when Winfield knocked Eckersley over with a smash to the mound and beat out the throw — which the Oakland ace tried to make from his backside.

The play of the game was turned in by Kelly Gruber, who dived across third base to grab a smash by Carney Lansford that was headed into the left-field corner. As it was, the A's scored a pair. Without Gruber's Gold Glove grab, it might have been a monster of an inning.

Guzman got the win, his second career post-season victory in as many tries. But it wasn't very tidy — seven hits and two runs in six innings with as many walks as strikeouts, three of each.

RON BULL

JUAN GUZMAN (LEFT) POURS IN ANOTHER STRIKE, WHILE RELIEVER DENNIS ECKERSLEY (ABOVE) TRIES TO THROW OUT WINFIELD AFTER BIG DAVE KNOCKED HIM OVER WITH SMASH TO THE MOUND.

RON BULL

'IN YOUR FACE,' SAYS PAT BORDERS AS McGWIRE TRIES TO BOWL HIM OVER AT THE PLATE IN KEY PLAY OF THE GAME. McGWIRE GOES FLYING AND UMPIRE AL CLARK MAKES IT OFFICIAL.

Juan up!

BLUE JAYS 7 at ATHLETICS 5
Game Three

Toronto	ab	r	h	bi	bb	so	avg.
White cf	3	0	1	0	2	0	.222
RAlomar 2b	5	1	1	1	0	0	.250
Carter rf	5	0	1	0	0	1	.167
Winfield dh	4	2	1	1	1	0	.273
Olerud 1b	5	1	1	0	0	1	.182
Maldonado lf	3	1	2	2	1	0	.222
Gruber 3b	4	0	0	0	0	1	.182
Borders c	4	1	1	0	0	1	.273
Lee ss	3	1	1	2	1	0	.250
Totals	36	7	9	6	5	4	

Oakland	ab	r	h	bi	bb	so	avg.
RHenderson lf	4	1	1	0	1	0	.100
Lansford 3b	5	0	1	0	0	0	.077
Sierra rf	4	1	2	2	0	0	.273
Baines dh	5	2	2	1	0	2	.538
McGwire 1b	4	0	1	0	0	1	.182
Steinbach c	4	0	3	2	1	0	.417
WWilson cf	4	0	2	0	1	1	.333
Bordick 2b	2	0	0	0	0	0	.000
a-Browne ph	0	0	0	0	1	0	—
1-Blankenship pr-2b	1	0	1	0	0	0	.333
Weiss ss	4	1	0	0	0	0	.167
Totals	37	5	13	5	4	4	

Toronto	010	110	211—7	9	1
Oakland	000	200	210—5	13	3

a—walked for Bordick in the 6th.
1—ran for Browne in the 6th.
E—Lee (1), Lansford (1), Blankenship 2 (2). LOB—Toronto 7, Oakland 11. 2B—White (1), Sierra (1). 3B—Lee (1). HR—RAlomar (1) off Darling, Maldonado (1) off Darling. RBIs—RAlomar (1), Winfield (2), Maldonado 2 (2), Lee 2 (3), Sierra 2 (2), Baines (3), Steinbach 2 (3). SB—Carter (2), RHenderson (1), WWilson 2 (6). CS—White (2), Maldonado (1). SF—Sierra. GIDP—RAlomar, Sierra.

Toronto	ip	h	r	er	bb	so	np	era
JuGuzman W, 1-0	6	7	2	2	3	3	104	3.00
DWard	1	3	2	2	1	1	29	18.00
Timlin	⅓	2	1	1	0	0	9	27.00
Henke S, 2	1⅔	1	0	0	0	0	13	0.00

Oakland	ip	h	r	er	bb	so	np	era
Darling L, 0-1	6	4	3	2	3	3	92	3.00
Downs	1	2	2	0	0	0	23	0.00
Corsi	⅓	0	0	0	0	0	2	0.00
JeRussell	⅔	1	2	2	3	0	29	18.00
Honeycutt	⅔	0	0	0	0	0	6	0.00
Eckersley	⅓	2	0	0	0	1	15	0.00

How the runs scored

Blue Jays' second: Winfield reached on an error, took third on a wild-pitch and scored when Maldonado singled. **Blue Jays 1, Athletics 0.**

Blue Jays' fourth: Alomar opened with a homer to left. **Blue Jays 2, Athletics 0.**

Athletics' fourth: Sierra led off with a double. Baines singled, scoring Sierra. McGwire was hit by a pitch, Baines to second. Steinbach singled to right, scoring Baines. **Blue Jays 2, Athletics 2.**

Blue Jays' fifth: Maldonado homered. **Blue Jays 3, Athletics 2.**

Blue Jays' seventh: Olerud reached on an error by second baseman Blankenship. With two down, Borders singled Olerud to second. Lee tripled down the line in right, scoring Olerud and Borders. **Blue Jays 5, Athletics 2.**

Athletics' seventh: Henderson took a lead-off walk, stole second and went to third on an error charged to Lee. With one out, Sierra scored Henderson with a sac fly to foul territory in right. Baines and McGwire singled, Baines holding at second. Steinbach singled to left, scoring Baines. **Blue Jays 5, Athletics 4.**

Blue Jays' eighth: Alomar grounded out and Russell came in to pitch. With two down, Winfield walked. Olerud singled to right, Winfield to third. Russell's first pitch to Maldonado skipped to the backstop, scoring Winfield. **Blue Jays 6, Athletics 4.**

Athletics' eighth: Blankenship led off with a single, but was forced at second on a fielder's choice by Weiss. Henderson singled to centre, Weiss to second. Henke relieved Timlin. Lansford flied to left. Sierra singled to right, scoring Weiss. **Blue Jays 6, Athletics 5.**

Blue Jays' ninth: Lee walked. Scored on Carter and Winfield singles. **Blue Jays 7, Athletics 5.**

JAYS STAGE BIGGEST COMEBACK IN TEAM HISTORY

GAME 4

Jays 7 at A's 6

It began in glorious sunshine, transformed itself in the long October shadows and ended in a blaze of autumn glory.

For Roberto Alomar and the Blue Jays, it was the finest hour.

For Dennis Eckersley and the Oakland A's, it was the day the bubble burst.

Yes, some legends were born and battered in this pivotal game, and the first to go was Jack Morris.

Before the first pitch was thrown, Jays fans were filled with optimism, and not just because of the fine Thanksgiving weekend

sunshine.

The previous day, their heroes had bested the A's 7-5 to take a 2-1 lead in the series. Today, they have Morris, Mr. Clutch, going against a questionable Bob Welch.

Well, Mr. Clutch slipped badly. In trouble early but escaping damage via an outstanding double play in the first, Morris carried a 1-0 lead into the third, thanks to a John Olerud homer.

Then came the inning from hell. Back-to-back-to-back singles by Mike Bordick, Lance Blankenship and Rickey Henderson, and we're tied. Four straight balls to Jerry Browne and it's bases loaded, nobody out.

Okay, Jack. Bear down, buddy. Oops! Sacrifice fly by Ruben Sierra and it's 2-1. Pitching coach Galen Cisco trots to the mound. Hey, Jack is *grinning* out there. Why?

Throwing 20 of 30 pitches out of the strike zone, nearly

JUMPING FOR JOY, ROBBIE ALOMAR LEAVES THE PLATE AFTER SMASHING HOMER THAT TIED THE GAME.   MIKE SLAUGHTER

Eck of a win!

BLUE JAYS 7 at ATHLETICS 6
Game Four

Toronto	ab	r	h	bi	bb	so	avg.
White cf	6	1	2	0	0	3	.267
RAlomar 2b	5	2	4	2	1	0	.412
Carter rf-1b	6	1	2	1	0	0	.222
Winfield dh	6	1	1	0	0	0	.235
Olerud 1b	5	1	4	2	0	1	.375
1-DBell pr-rf	0	1	0	0	1	0	—
Maldonado lf	5	0	2	1	1	1	.286
Gruber 3b	5	0	0	1	1	1	.125
Borders c	5	0	1	1	0	0	.250
Lee ss	3	0	1	0	0	1	.273
a-Sprague ph	1	0	0	0	0	1	.500
Griffin ss	2	0	0	0	0	0	.000
Totals	49	7	17	7	4	8	

Oakland	ab	r	h	bi	bb	so	avg.
RHenderson lf	6	2	3	1	0	0	.250
Browne cf	2	1	0	0	1	0	.000
WWilson cf	2	0	0	0	0	0	.286
Sierra rf	4	0	2	2	1	1	.333
Baines dh	5	1	2	1	0	0	.500
2-Fox pr-dh	1	0	0	0	0	0	.000
McGwire 1b	4	0	0	1	1	1	.133
Steinbach c	4	0	1	1	1	1	.313
Lansford 3b	5	0	2	1	0	0	.167
Bordick ss	5	1	1	0	0	0	.077
Blankenship 2b	4	1	2	0	1	1	.429
Totals	42	6	12	6	5	4	

Toronto	010	000	032	01—7	17	4
Oakland	005	001	000	00—6	12	2

a-struck out for Lee in the 8th.
1-ran for Olerud in the 9th. 2-ran for Baines in the 9th.

E—White (1), Borders (1), Lee 2 (3), RHenderson (2), McGwire (1). LOB—Toronto 14, Oakland 11. 2B—RAlomar (1), Olerud (1), Sierra (2), Baines (1). HR—RAlomar (2) off Eckersley, Olerud (1) off Welch. RBIs—RAlomar 2 (3), Carter (1), Olerud 2 (3), Maldonado (3), Borders (2), RHenderson (1), Sierra 2 (4), Baines (4), Steinbach (4), Lansford (1). SB—RAlomar (3), RHenderson (2), Fox (1), Blankenship (1). S—Browne, McGwire. SF—Borders, Sierra. GIDP—Baines, Bordick.

Toronto	ip	h	r	er	bb	so	np	era
JaMorris	3 1/3	5	5	5	2	67	6.57	
Stottlemyre	3 2/3	3	1	1	0	1	47	2.45
Timlin	1	2	0	0	0	1	17	6.75
DWard W, 1-0	2	1	0	0	0	0	15	6.00
Henke S, 3	1	1	0	0	0	0	13	0.00

Oakland	ip	h	r	er	bb	so	np	era
Welch	7	7	2	2	1	7	121	2.57
Parrett	0	2	2	2	0	0	8	54.00
Eckersley	1 2/3	5	2	2	0	1	41	6.00
Corsi	1	2	0	0	2	0	29	0.00
Downs L, 0-1	1 1/3	1	1	1	1	0	24	3.86

How the runs scored

Jays' second' Welch pitching. With one out, Olerud hit a wrong-field homer to left. Maldonado and Gruber both flied out to deep centre. **Blue Jays 1, Athletics 0.**

A's third: Morris pitching. Boridck led off with a single, moved up on a single by Blankenship and scored on a single by Henderson, Blankenship to second. Browne walked, loading the bases. Sierra scored Blankenship with a sac fly to right, Henderson taking third. Baines doubled to left, scoring Henderson and moving Browne to third. McGwire was walked intentionally to load the bases. Steinbach walked on four pitches, forcing in Browne. Lansford beat out an infield chopper to shortstop, scoring Baines. **Athletics 5, Blue Jays 1.**

A's sixth: Stottlemyre pitching. With one out, Henderson singled, stole second and went to third on Browne's ground-out to second. Sierra doubled to right, scoring Henderson. **Athletics 6, Blue Jays 1.**

Jays' eighth: Welch gave up a leadoff double to Alomar and Parrett came in to pitch. Carter singled home Alomar. Winfield singled Carter to third and Eckersley came in to pitch. Olerud singled off the first pitch, scoring Carter and moving Winfield to third. Maldonado singled off the next pitch, scoring Winfield. **Athletics 6, Blue Jays 4.**

Jays' ninth: White led off with a single to left, going all the way to third when Henderson overran the ball. Alomar homered to right. **Blue Jays 6, Athletics 6.**

Jays' 11th: Downs pitching. Bell led off with a walk, moving to third on Maldonado's bloop single to right. Gruber lined to first. Borders scored Bell with a sac liner to left. **Blue Jays 7, Athletics 6.**

RICK EGLINTON

UNHAPPY ECK DELIVERS PITCH AFTER PITCH IN GAME 4 AND SEES THEM ALL COME BACK HIS WAY — FOR FOUR RUNS.

DEREK BELL SLIDES INTO THIRD IN THE 11TH AND, ONE OUT LATER, SCORED THE WINNING RUN.

RON BULL

66

beaning Carney Lansford and almost unleashing a pickoff throw into the stands, Morris clearly had nothing but his reputation going for him. By now, millions of Jays fans watching and listening at home are screaming those three little words: *TAKE HIM OUT!*

Cito never leaves the dugout. When the carnage ends, Oakland has batted around and it's 5-1. When Todd Stottlemyre (who finally replaced Morris in the fourth) surrenders another run in the sixth, it seems to be over.

Welch is pitching well and Blue Jays hopes are in intensive care, ready to receive the last rites. But wait. There's still a faint pulse in the eighth inning. Time to call in Dr. Alomar.

Wham! It's a double down the right-field line by Alomar and Welch is gone. Then singles by Joe Carter and Dave Winfield off Jeff Parrett. Now it's 6-2 and . . .

Uh, oh! Here comes the Eck, and you *know* it's over. The major leagues' premier reliever has allowed only two of 31 baserunners to score this year and . . .

Crack! Hey, a single by Olerud on the first pitch, and that's

RON BULL

a run. Gee, you don't expect . . .

Crack! Another single by Candy Maldonado on the next pitch, and *another* run! What *is* this?

Back home, fans who'd sat down to Sunday dinner are being called back to their TVs and radios. Eck had worked the day before and gave up a run. Now he's in an inning early, has already given up two and has runners on second and third with Ed Sprague at the plate. If only Sprague could . . .

Nah! Eckersley strikes him out, pumping his fist in triumph. He still has a two-run lead.

It's the ninth now. Last chance. More of us have drifted back to the TV, just in time to be reminded Oakland has an 81-1 record entering the ninth with a lead.

Crack! Devon White singles to left. Rickey Henderson over-runs the ball and White's on third. Dr. Alomar! Calling Dr. Alomar!

CRAACKKK! Now comes a sequence of images some of us will carry in our minds forever.

The long shadows reaching out beyond the plate. Soft sunshine glinting off Eckersley's droopy black moustache. Sierra going back, *baaack* in right field. Stopping at the wall. Looking up as the ball soars over. Tony La Russa alone on the bench, head down.

And wonderful Robbie Alomar, fingers raised in triumph, 4 for 4, circling the bases, jumping on the plate with both feet. Tie game.

Shhh! Did you hear a pop? The Eckersley mystique.

But it wasn't over, was it? Oh, noooo.

Duane Ward, roughed up the previous day, surrenders a leadoff single to Harold Baines. Eric Fox, running for Baines, steals second, then moves to third on a fine sacrifice bunt by slugger Mark McGwire, the fourth of his career.

Now the winning run is on third, one out. A sacrifice fly would tie it. Dangerous Terry Steinbach at the plate. Jays infield drawn in. Ward delivers a hellacious fastball, low on the outside corner. Steinbach swings and hits a sharp grounder . . . right to Alomar, who fires to Pat Borders at home to tag the impetuous Fox for the second out.

Whew! Another grounder from Lansford and we're into extra innings. Hey, is anybody gonna eat this dinner? It's getting cold!

As the game enters its fourth hour, the shadows are creeping to the edge of the diamond-patterned outfield grass. Finally, in the top of the 11th, Kelly Downs walks Derek Bell and Maldonado comes through with a single.

When McGwire spears a Gruber liner to save a run, it looks as if dinner will have to wait indefinitely. But a Borders sacrifice fly cashes Bell, and the Jays have the lead at last.

Tom Henke, out for his third save in the series, makes no mistake in the bottom of the 11th, retiring Baines, Fox and McGwire to put his team on the threshold of history.

Was this four-hour, 25-minute roller coaster the most memorable Blue Jays game ever? To this point, yes. But there is more to come.

ROCKED EARLY IN GAME 4, JACK MORRIS WATCHES FROM THE BENCH AS THE JAYS STAGE THEIR BIG COMEBACK.

RICKEY RUNS THE JAYS OUT OF TOWN

GAME 5

Jays 2 at A's 7

Rickey Henderson couldn't wait to get another crack at David Cone, the pitcher with the worst record in the majors for holding runners.

He got his chance in Game 5 of the American League playoffs and made the most of it. In fact, Rickey managed to rattle Cone, the outfielders, the infielders and bench coach Gene Tenace.

When the dust from his dives and slides had settled, the result was a 6-2 win by the Athletics to stave off elimination and send the series back to Toronto.

Cone's problems with Rickey began in the third inning. The Jays were down 2-0, on a Ruben Sierra home run, and the fireballer had just walked Henderson on a close 3-and-2 pitch. He threw over a couple of times to hold Rickey close, then whirled and hurled the ball away.

By the time the Jays had recovered it, Rickey was filing his nails at third. He scored easily on the first of four hits by the Governor, Jerry Browne, filling in at third for a bruised and battered Carney Lansford. That run was all the A's would need to beat the Jays in this one.

A lot of credit for that went to Dave Stewart, making his second fine start of the series. The victory upped his championship series record for the A's to a remarkable 6-0.

Stewart is nobody's fool. He had witnessed the devastation that had taken place in Game 4, when the Jays got into Oakland's relief pitching pantry, so he made sure that didn't happen to him.

Giving each batter in turn his menacing death stare, Stewart went an unrelenting nine innings, holding the Jays to just seven hits. His one big mistake was a pitch on the outside of the plate to Dave Winfield in the fourth inning, after three of his inside offerings had been called balls. He didn't even have to turn his head to know where Winfield had put that one, making the score 3-1.

It looked like it might be a game after all, and visions of another comeback were dancing off manager Cito Gaston's cool shades — until Rickey and his gang came up in the fifth, that is.

Lance Blankenship started things off with a smash to third that Kelly Gruber booted for a field goal to left. Blankenship got all the way to second before Gruber caught up with the

LEFT: DAVE STEWART USES HIS DEATH STARE AND A WICKED FORKBALL TO SILENCE THE JAYS IN GAME 5.

RIGHT: RICKEY MAKES A REAL PEST OF HIMSELF IN GAME 5, RUNNING LIKE THE STOLEN BASE KING OF OLD.

RICK EGLINTON

MIKE SLAUGHTER

In a stew!

BLUE JAYS 2 at ATHLETICS 6
Game Five

Toronto	ab	r	h	bi	bb	so	avg.
White cf	4	0	3	1	0	0	.368
RAlomar 2b	4	0	1	0	0	0	.381
Carter rf	3	0	0	0	1	1	.190
Winfield dh	3	1	2	1	1	0	.300
Olerud 1b	4	0	0	0	0	3	.300
Maldonado lf	4	0	0	0	0	0	.222
Gruber 3b	3	1	0	0	1	0	.105
Borders c	4	0	1	0	0	0	.250
Lee ss	3	0	0	0	1	1	.214
Totals	32	2	7	2	3	5	
Oakland	ab	r	h	bi	bb	so	avg.
RHenderson lf	3	2	2	0	1	0	.316
1-Fox pr-lf	0	0	0	0	0	0	.000
Browne 3b	4	2	4	2	0	0	.667
Sierra rf	4	1	2	3	0	0	.368
Baines dh	3	0	0	0	0	1	.429
McGwire 1b	1	0	0	0	3	1	.125
Steinbach c	4	0	0	0	0	1	.250
WWilson cf	4	0	0	0	0	0	.222
Bordick ss	4	0	0	0	0	0	.059
Blankenship 2b	4	1	0	0	0	1	.273
Totals	31	6	8	5	4	4	

Toronto	000	100	100—2	7	3
Oakland	201	030	00x—6	8	0

1-ran for R.Henderson in the 7th.
E—Carter (1), Gruber (1), Cone (1). LOB—Toronto 6, Oakland 6. 2B—White (2). HR—Sierra (1) off Cone, Winfield (2) off Stewart. RBIs—White (1), Winfield (3), Browne 2 (2), Sierra 3 (7). CS—White (3), Sierra (2). S—Baines.
  Runners left in scoring position—Toronto 2 (RAlomar, Olerud); Oakland 3 (McGwire, Steinbach 2).
  Runners moved up—Sierra, Baines.
  DP—Oakland 1 (Blankenship and Bordick).

Toronto	ip	h	r	er	bb	so	np	era
Cone L, 1-1	4	6	6	3	2	3	80	3.00
Key	3	2	0	0	2	1	40	0.00
Eichhorn	1	0	0	0	0	0	11	0.00
Oakland	ip	h	r	er	bb	so	np	era
Stewart W, 1-0	9	7	2	2	3	5	139	2.70

Cone pitched to 4 batters in the 5th; Inherited runners–scored—Key 1-0; IBB—off Key (McGwire) 1. PB—Borders; Umpires—Home, Brinkman; First, Coble; Second, Denkinger; Third, Young; Left, Clark; Right, Merrill; T—2:51. A—44,955.

How the runs scored

Athletics' first: Cone pitching. Henderson flew out to centre. Browne singled sharply to right. Sierra drilled a 1-1 pitch over the fence in right for a home run, also scoring Browne. Baines flew out to centre. McGwire walked. Steinbach took a called strike three. **Athletics 2, Blue Jays 0.**

Athletics' third: Henderson led off with a walk and took third on Cone's throwing error. Browne singled to centre, driving in Henderson. With Sierra batting, Borders' passed ball allowed Browne to take second. Sierra flew out to centre; Browne to third. Baines struck out. McGwire struck out. **Athletics 3, Blue Jays 0.**

Jays' fourth: Stewart pitching. Winfield led off by driving a 3-1 pitch to left-centre for his second homer of the series. Olerud took a called third strike. Maldonado popped to second. Gruber popped foul to third. **Athletics 3, Blue Jays 1.**

Athletics' fifth: Blankenship, leading off, was safe on Gruber's two-base fielding error. Henderson beat out a bunt single to the left side; Blankenship to third. Browne singled to right, scoring Blankenship; Henderson to third; Carter's throwing error allowed Henderson to score and Browne to take third. Sierra singled to centre, scoring Browne. Key replaced Cone. Baines' sacrifice bunt advanced Sierra to second. McGwire was walked intentionally. With Steinbach up, Sierra thrown out trying to steal, catcher to third. Steinbach grounded into a fielder's choice, short to second. **Athletics 6, Blue Jays 1.**

Jays' seventh: Gruber led off by drawing a walk. Borders singled to right; Gruber to third. Lee struck out. White singled to centre, scoring Gruber; Borders to second. Alomar lined out to second and Borders was doubled up, second to short. **Athletics 6, Blue Jays 2.**

ball. Then Cone found himself facing that pest Henderson one more time.

The gimpy speedster — held to 48 steals this year because of injuries that kept him out of more than 40 games — made a perfect bunt toward third. It was Cone's play because Gruber had to keep Blankenship from advancing. By the time the pitcher got to the ball, Rickey was well across first base.

Then Browne drove another hit to right, with Joe Carter and Gruber messing up an attempt to nail Rickey at third as Blankenship scored. The ball bounced away and Henderson had produced another unearned run. Cone, who had lost his trademark cool, gave up another hit to Sierra, which scored Browne, before odd-man-out Jimmy Key came in to put out the fire.

Rickey wasn't through yet. In the seventh, he was at the plate again and appeared to swing at a breaking pitch from Key. When the umpires decided he hadn't gone around, Tenace bolted out of the dugout and was ejected from the game.

Henderson, enjoying the carnage he was creating, celebrated by driving another hit past shortstop Manuel Lee before giving way to a pinch runner.

Fans watching back home were reminded of general manager Pat Gillick's warning to the Jays before the playoffs started: Keep Rickey off base, or expect the worst. They didn't,

and it happened.

Jays pitching was almost perfect past the first three men in the order; Henderson, Browne and Sierra had all eight of Oakland's hits.

Really optimistic fans were still hopeful when the Jays came up for the sixth, down by five runs. After all, that was the same margin they had bounced back from in the previous game, and they had set off those fireworks a lot later.

But all the Jays could manage was a run in the seventh, when Gruber, who had walked, scored on Devon White's third hit of the game.

The Jays made few excuses. Cone said, "I just couldn't establish my fastball and it cost me."

What about seven errors in two games? Some Jays hinted that the field wasn't in good shape after a Guns n' Roses rock concert.

The contest wasn't over long before second-guessers loudly reviewed the team's playoff pitching plans. Why not a four-man rotation including Key, who had won his last five decisions? Jack Morris in Game 4, and Cone in this one, pitched as if they could have used another day's rest. And Key was almost perfect in his relief appearance.

Thank goodness the young arm of Juan Guzman was up next. But he, too, had only three days' rest. Would any of the second-guessers suggest using someone else?

RON BULL

'LET'S NOT GET IN ANY MORE TROUBLE THAN WE ARE,' MANAGER CITO GASTON SAYS AS HE RESTRAINS BENCH COACH GENE TENACE FROM RUNNING ON TO THE FIELD.

JUAN-WAY TICKET TO THE SERIES

GAME 6

A's 2 at Jays 9

Bill Singer took the sign from Rick Cerone, rocked back and fired the first pitch past Ralph Garr of the Chicago White Sox. *Steeeerike!*

Now, 2,555 official American League games later, Juan Guzman takes the sign from Pat Borders, rocks back and fires the first pitch past Rickey Henderson of the Oakland A's. *Steeeerike!*

Took a while, didn't it? April 7, 1977 to Oct. 14, 1992. But, after 16 seasons and three unsuccessful playoffs, the Blue Jays are en route to the World Series.

That first pitch from Guzman,

ripping past Rickey with a sound like tearing silk, is their first-class ticket to Atlanta.

At the SkyDome, where late arrivals are still scooting in from the rain for the unusual 3 p.m. start, there's a tremendous cheer. Attaboy, Juan! Throw strikes!

Three pitches later, when Rickey lifts a harmless fly to Devon White in centre, there's an almost palpable sense of relief. The spark plug of the A's, who'd chalked up six hits and two walks in his last 12 at-bats while scoring five runs, is shuffling back to the bench.

When Jerry Browne (4 for 4 in Oakland's Game 5 victory) and Ruben Sierra (7 for 19 to this point) are dispatched quickly, the positive indicators are there for all to see:

Guzman, who'd clinched the divisional championship against Detroit 11 days earlier and won Game 3 in Oakland, looks strong and focused. He is working quickly, getting

RICK EGLINTON

PLAYOFF MVP ROBBIE ALOMAR GETS VICTORY HUG FROM GAME 6 WINNER JUAN GUZMAN.

ahead of the hitters and zeroing in on his target with a wicked slider and a fastball in the mid-90s.

Now, what can the Jays do with Oakland's winningest starter, Mike Moore? The answer isn't long in coming.

Remember? White sends a weak, opposite-field pop down the left-field line. Rickey jogs in to take it. The ball floats down to Rickey's glove and, *incredibly* . . . BOUNCES OUT!

What a break! While White — looking remarkably cool for a guy who'd been involved in the crackup of a $140,000 Mercedes the previous day — dances off second, the crowd begins a derisive chant which will be repeated many times this afternoon: *Rick-eeeey! Rick-eeeey!*

Now, after Roberto Alomar strikes out, we have Joe Carter (hitting a miserable .190 in the series) working Moore to a 2-and-2 count. Moore comes inside with a thigh-high fastball. Joe *swings* and launches a rainbow shot to dead centre.

Willie Wilson is drifting back . . . to the warning track . . . the fence . . . he *leaps* . . . but that ball is *GONE!*

In the SkyDome, maple leaf flags are waving while the loudest cheer ever heard at a Canadian sports event is drowning out the fireworks. In homes and workplaces across the country, millions of Canadians are smiling, laughing, screaming.

RON BULL

Daring to hope. Daring to dream: "Yes! *This* time. *This could be it!*"

In the top of the third, we're not so sure. With only one out, Guzman has just walked Lance Blankenship. Wilson is on second and Rickey is strutting to the plate.

Once again, the man who'd murdered the Jays in the '89 playoffs has a chance to be the spoiler — but not today. In five pitches, the Destroyer is destroyed, waving feebly at a devil's brew of high heat and fadeaway breakers. *Rick-eeey! Rick-eeey!*

Browne fails to get the ball out of the infield, and Oakland's only real threat of the day is snuffed.

Fifteen minutes later, the cake is ready and the Candy Man has the icing. With one run already in, Candy Maldonado is coming to the plate with Dave Winfield on third, John Olerud on second.

The 1-and-1 pitch from Moore. Good-*BYE!* Candy meets it on the sweet spot and jolts Mr. Rawlings into the second deck in right-centre. The scoreboard reads 6-0.

The rest of the afternoon has a feeling of New Year's Eve. A lot of happy people gabbing, watching and waiting. A little anxious, perhaps. Anxious to celebrate.

In the fifth, Terry Stienbach finally gets the first A's hit, and Guzman is nicked for a run in the sixth. But when Juan leaves after seven with eight strikeouts, there is no doubt: He (not Jack Morris or David Cone) has been the Jays' dominant pitcher of this series. Some even link his name with Koufax.

The dominant player? After eight innings, Alomar will have lined three hits, stolen two bases and driven in another run to seal his status as playoff MVP. As the defiant A's come up for their last gasps in the ninth, most of the 51,335 celebrants are on their feet, as they have been for some time. Singing the Hey-Hey-Goodbye song, jeering Rickey (0 for 4), even chanting "We Want Eck!"

Appropriately, the last out is recorded by Maldonado, king for a day, taking Sierra's routine fly in the same neighborhood where Rickey had fluffed White's ball three hours earlier.

The long wait is over, and the Blow Jays are history.

KEN FAUGHT

ABOVE: RICKEY SHOWS UP TO CONGRATULATE CARTER.

LEFT: JUBILANT PAT BORDERS LEAPS INTO ARMS OF TOM HENKE AS JOHN OLERUD RUSHES TO JOIN IN.

BERNARD WEIL

ABOVE: FLAG-WAVING FAN RUSHES ON TO FIELD TO JOIN MANUEL LEE, LEFT, AND CANDY MALDONADO IN CELEBRATION.

LEFT: DAVE STIEB AND KELLY GRUBER ENJOY THE MOMENT.

RON BULL

What a blast!

ATHLETICS 2 at BLUE JAYS 9
Game Six

Oakland	ab	r	h	bi	bb	so	avg.
RHenderson lf	4	0	0	0	0	2	.261
c-Quirk ph	1	0	0	0	0	0	.000
Browne 3b	4	0	0	0	0	0	.400
Lansford 3b	0	0	0	0	0	1	.167
Sierra rf	5	1	1	0	0	0	.333
Baines dh	4	1	2	0	0	0	.440
McGwire 1b	4	0	1	1	0	0	.150
Steinbach c	4	0	2	1	0	2	.292
WWilson cf	4	0	1	0	0	3	.227
Bordick ss	2	0	0	0	0	1	.053
a-Fox ph	0	0	0	0	1	0	.000
Weiss ss	0	0	0	0	1	0	.167
Blankenship 2b	2	0	0	0	1	1	.231
b-Ready ph	1	0	0	0	0	1	.000
Totals	35	2	7	2	4	10	
Toronto	ab	r	h	bi	bb	so	avg.
White cf	4	1	1	1	0	1	.348
RAlomar 2b	5	1	3	1	0	1	.423
Carter rf	5	1	1	2	0	1	.192
Winfield dh	4	1	0	0	1	2	.250
Olerud 1b	3	2	2	1	1	0	.348
Maldonado lf	4	1	2	3	0	1	.273
Gruber 3b	3	0	0	0	0	1	.091
Borders c	2	1	2	1	1	0	.318
Lee ss	4	1	2	0	0	0	.278
Totals	34	9	13	9	3	7	

```
Oakland      000 001 010—2  7  1
Toronto      204 010 02x—9 13  0
```

a-walked for Bordick in the 7th. b-struck out for Blankenship in the 9th. c-flied out for R.Henderson in the 9th.

E—RHenderson (3). LOB—Oakland 10, Toronto 7. 2B—Baines (2), Olerud (2), Lee (1). HR—Carter (1) off Moore, Maldonado (2) off Moore. RBIs—McGwire (3), Steinbach (5), White (2), RAlomar (4), Carter 2 (3), Olerud (4), Maldonado 3 (6), Borders (3). SB—Sierra (1), WWilson (7), Fox (2), RAlomar 2 (5). CS—White (4). S—Gruber. SF—White, Borders.

Runners left in scoring position—Oakland 6 (RHenderson, Browne 2, Sierra, WWilson 2); Toronto 3 (White, Winfield, Lee).

Oakland	ip	h	r	er	bb	so	np	era
Moore L, 0–2	2 ⅔	7	6	5	1	4	50	7.45
Parrett	2	4	1	1	0	1	33	11.57
Honeycutt	1 ⅓	0	0	0	0	1	14	0.00
JeRussell	1	0	0	0	1	0	12	9.00
Witt	1	2	2	2	1	1	25	18.00
Toronto	ip	h	r	er	bb	so	np	era
JuGuzman W, 2–0	7	5	1	1	2	8	118	2.08
DWard	1	2	1	1	0	1	14	6.75
Henke	1	0	0	0	2	1	27	0.00

How the runs scored

Jays' first: Moore pitching. Leading off, White reached on a two-base error by Henderson in left. After Alomar struck out, Carter homered to centre on a 2-2 pitch. **Blue Jays 2, Athletics 0.**

Jays' third: Alomar led off with a single to centre, then stole second. After Carter struck out, Winfield was walked intentionally. Olerud hit a ground-rule double to right, scoring Alomar, while Winfield was obliged to hold at third. Maldonado homered to right-centre on a 1-1 pitch. **Blue Jays 6, Athletics 0.**

Jays' fifth: Parrett pitching. Olerud led off with a single past second, moving to second on Maldonado's single to centre. Gruber sacrificed both runners over and Borders scored Olerud with a sac fly to left. **Blue Jays 7, Athletics 0.**

A's sixth: Guzman pitching. With one out, Sierra singled, then stole second. Baines singled Sierra to third. McGwire singled, scoring Sierra. **Blue Jays 7, Athletics 1.**

A's eighth: Ward on to pitch for Guzman. Sierra flied out but Baines followed with a double to left-centre. McGwire grounded to third, Baines holding. Steinbach singled to score Baines. Wilson struck out. **Blue Jays 7, Athletics 2.**

Jays' eighth: Witt pitching. Borders opened with a walk, going to third on Lee's double to left. White scored Borders with a sac fly to right. Alomar singled, scoring Lee. **Blue Jays 9, Athletics 2.**

BRAVE NEW WORLD

The World Series and Toronto's in it. Words to savor. Ideas to let loose in your head. A time to do something crazy, like giving your newborn baby girl Alomar for a middle name. Or getting the Blue Jays symbol clipped into your hair, as Joe Carter and Devon White did. A time to enjoy — no questions asked.

But for baseball fans, that kind of feeling has about a two-day lifespan. Then the questions start flooding in and screaming for answers.

Who are these guys standing between the Blue Jays and the promised land?

Would Jane Fonda be at the SkyDome? And would she be able to stay awake for the whole game?

Would Jimmy Key get a chance to pitch?

Who would be benched with no DH in the games played in Atlanta?

Would any of the Jays' pitchers bat without doing the team — or themselves — serious injury?

The first question was the only toughie. The answer to Fonda was yes and no. The answer to Key was yes, since manager Cito Gaston had pencilled him in to pitch Game 4 at the SkyDome. Simple mathematics told us that meant Juan Guzman would pitch not only Game 3 but Game 7 (if there was one), a thought that made every fan north of the 49th parallel very happy.

It was also announced that Dave Winfield would start in right field in Atlanta, meaning hot-hitting John Olerud would be the odd man out in Game 1 against the Braves' crafty, but ailing, lefty Tom Glavine.

Frankly, the Jays pitchers were expected to go zero for the series at the plate, except for David Cone who in 1989 was the top NL hitter among pitchers, with 18. But even if they did nothing at the plate in Atlanta, the Jays' pitchers wouldn't be far behind their Brave counterparts, who posted a .165 batting average during '92.

Now, what about that first question: Just who are these guys, anyway? How did they match up against the Jays?

Although the two teams had never met in mortal combat, the Atlanta Braves were not exactly strangers.

Every Jays fan knew Bobby Cox, for sure: the platoon sergeant, the feisty skipper who had led Toronto out of the wilderness and into the playoffs in 1985. Now, he was doing the same for the Atlanta Braves for the second year in a row. In '91, he had taken them from last to first, and taken the Minnesota Twins to the 10th inning of the seventh game of the World Series before succumbing one-zip.

From what we remembered of him, he liked two guys playing each base — not at the same time, of course. And we always believed he would have pinch hit for Ted Williams in the bottom of the ninth if the other team had thrown a lefty at him. But no one who knew anything about the game doubted his ability to get the most out of the hand he was dealt.

Then there was Jeff Reardon, the major league leader in career saves, who set the record while playing for the faltering Red Sox. His trade to the National League seemed to have given him new life, but people knew he was no longer a stopper in the same league with Tom Henke.

Francisco Cabrera, we gave them. If we hadn't, we would be playing the Pittsburgh Pirates. This 26-year-old catcher, sent south in one of those Jim Acker revolving-door trades, was a late-season emergency replacement for the injured Greg Olson. Cabrera was the answer to a trivia question before he stroked the dramatic, two-out single in the bottom of the ninth that broke every heart in Pittsburgh.

Most of us had seen the other Braves only on TV, where they had commanded almost as much prime time as *Murphy Brown* in '91 and '92. Twenty-one post-season games in two years . . . and counting.

Twice we had seen them beat the Pirates in dramatic, seven-game series. Last year, we watched longingly as they took the Minnesota Twins — and Jack Morris — to the edge.

The Braves' cast was much the same for their second taste of the whole enchilada. But in matching them up with the Jays, you had to be careful with the clues being offered, such as the one that showed the Jays had a big edge in almost every important category.

The Jays had outhit the Braves (.263 to .254), scored more

runs (780 to 667), driven in more runs (737 to 628), hit more homers (163 to 136), stolen more bases (129 to 125), struck out more batters (954 to 920) and produced more saves (49 to 40).

But the season's offensive statistics weren't nearly as meaningful as they appeared. Instead of a pitcher fanning or popping out every ninth at-bat or so, which happens in the National League, the Jays had Winfield driving in 108 runs, scoring 92 and slamming 26 homers from the DH slot. The entire Atlanta pitching staff had driven in 21 runs, scored 31 and produced one long ball. They also struck out 117 times in 364 at-bats.

Position-by-position comparisons were also made more difficult before Game 1 by Cox's reliance, by choice or necessity, on platooning. Take first base, for example. Olerud had locked up that position with the Jays until the DH problem reared its ugly head in the Series. Meanwhile, Sid Bream and Brian Hunter shared first base duties for Atlanta, producing an impressive 24 homers and 102 RBIs between them.

Cox also platooned catchers Greg Olson and Damon Berryhill, and shortstops Jeff Blauser (good hit) and Rafael Belliard (better glove). With Olson out for the Series because of injury, Berryhill was thought to be on his own until Cabrera's key hit in the NL playoffs.

One place where everyone gave the Braves a big edge was at third base, where switch-hitting all-star Terry Pendleton, a product of the Kirby Puckett body building school, had batted .311 and tied for the NL lead with 199 hits. He also clubbed 21 homers and drove in 105, more than any other Jay except Carter and Winfield. Kelly Gruber was in that league back in 1990, but this season, plagued again by injuries, only compared with Pendleton as a fielder — and even there, Gruber's edge wasn't tremendous.

Before the first game of the Series, Star baseball writer Allan Ryan gave the Jays a wide edge at second because of Robbie Alomar. At 24, Alomar was considered by some, including A's reliever Dennis Eckersley, to be the best player in baseball. But nobody took counterpart Mark Lemke (who hit .417 in the '91 Series) lightly.

Ryan also gave the Jays a distinct edge at DH, Winfield against anyone Cox sent up; in right, where Carter was matched with Dave Justice, who had 47 fewer RBIs; in centre, where Devon White has no rival as a fielder and was hitting as well as Otis Nixon; and at catcher, where Pat Borders, who had caught more games than anyone else in the AL during the season, was up against a part-time player with a .228 average.

Ryan called it even at three positions: short, with Manuel Lee getting an edge in the field and Blauser at the plate; left field, where Candy Maldonado and fleet Ron Gant produced good stats during the season and played key roles in the playoffs; and first base, when Olerud was paired with Bream, who is a good fielder but had six fewer homers and five fewer RBIs.

One of the best, and most controversial, Braves would start the Series on the bench. Neon Deion Sanders, who was combining baseball with football (the Atlanta Falcons), had hit .304 in sporadic play.

Pitching, despite the disarray of Atlanta's starters in the playoffs, was a plus for the National Leaguers — at least on paper. The Atlanta staff had a distinctive team ERA of 3.14, compared with the Jays' leaky 3.91. But ERA is also a misleading stat when comparing the two leagues. NL pitchers face their mound rival every ninth batter or so, while AL pitchers get heavy-hitting DHs, instead.

But there was no denying '91 Cy Young winner Glavine had demonstrated again that he is one of the best pitchers in baseball when his ribs are right. He was 20-8 with an ERA of 2.76. Glavine won one game fewer than Morris, but gave up more than one run fewer per game, on average.

Atlanta's No. 2 starter, scheduled to face David Cone, was John Smoltz (15-12 and 2.85 during the season). With a behavioral psychologist helping him to stay focused, the right-handed power pitcher was Atlanta's toughest thrower through the second half and was the MVP in the playoffs. He doesn't fan as many as Cone does, but edged him as NL strikeout king after the former Met was traded to the Jays.

The weakest of the Atlanta big three was Steve Avery (11-11 and 3.20). He had an off-year and a bad playoff. Scouts said when catcher Olson suffered a dislocated ankle, it hurt Avery badly. He depended on Olson to call the game. Avery against Juan Guzman (16-5 and 2.64 ERA) seemed like the mismatch of the Series.

Mike Stanton had emerged as the ace of the Atlanta bullpen, despite the addition of Reardon. But the Braves had no closers as reliable as Duane Ward and Henke, so the bullpen was a big Toronto plus.

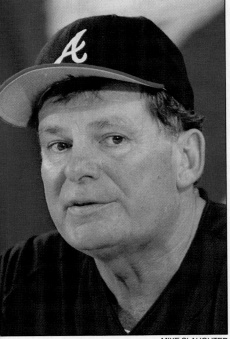

MIKE SLAUGHTER

ATLANTA SKIPPER BOBBY COX LED TORONTO OUT OF THE WILDERNESS IN 1985.

MIKE SLAUGHTER

TORONTO STAR T-SHIRTS APPEAR IN ATLANTA ON GARY ANDERSON AND HELENE DAVIAU.

WILD MORRIS MADE ONE MISTAKE TOO MANY

GAME 1

Jays 1 at **Braves 3**

Jack Morris was Jack Morris, but Tom Glavine was brilliant.

Those were the two most important factors in a 3-1 Braves victory that ruined the Blue Jays' World Series debut in Game 1 at Atlanta-Fulton County Stadium.

For five innings, Morris was as good as he gets. His split-fingered fastball (a.k.a. forkball) was working like the $5 million charm it is. It had every Brave so off-balance that seven of them had already fanned.

Torontonians had watched that pitch with admiration all season long, hitters lunging at thin air as the bottom fell out just as the forkball arrived at the plate. It's that wonderful dip that makes every Jack Morris pitch worth about $1,300 on the big-league market.

For Morris, at 37, and with 3,000 innings on his arm, the splitter is his livelihood. Without it, there would be no 21 victories in '92, no four World Series wins in other years. He uses it to get a favorable count on batters, and he uses it to finish them off.

In his last World Series appearance, it had carried him through the 10-inning, seventh-game shutout that made champions out of the Minnesota Twins. In fact, Jack had closed to within one of Hall of Famer Bob Gibson's Series record of 19 scoreless innings as he struck out shortstop Jeff Blauser to end the fifth.

But Jack was living on the edge as he trudged to the mound to start the sixth. In the previous two innings, he had retired the first two batters and then walked the next two. In the playoffs, it had become clear to fans watching Morris struggle that he who lives by the splitter dies by the splitter when wildness enters the equation.

Which brings us to the bottom of the sixth inning of a first-rate pitching duel — the first time two 20-game winners had gone head to head since 1969 (Tom Seaver vs. Mike Cuellar). Joe Carter has given the Jays a 1-0 lead with a homer deep into the left-field stands to start the fourth inning. Jack, after a good rest following his playoff disasters, was looking like vintage Morris again, especially after he got Terry Pendleton, the Braves' best hitter, to bounce out to Robbie Alomar to start the inning.

Next, Morris is ready to put cleanup hitter David Justice away with his prized pitch, but misses on a 3-and-2 count.

Not to worry. Justice is no threat to steal and the batter, Sid Bream, is no threat to hit; he's never touched Morris in 11 World Series tries. But this time, Bream slaps a single between short and third. Manager Cito Gaston is worried enough that he has Todd Stottlemyre working in the bullpen.

JEFF GOODE

GOODBYE, MR RAWLINGS. JOE CARTER GIVES JAYS 1-0 LEAD WITH HOMER DEEP TO LEFT.

MIKE SLAUGHTER

JEFF GOODE

THERE GOES THE BALL GAME! JACK MORRIS SHOWS HIS DISGUST AS DAMON
BERRYHILL ROUNDS BASES AFTER GAME-WINNING HOMER. DAVID JUSTICE AND
RON GANT, WHO WERE ON BASE, CONGRATULATE THEIR UNLIKELY HERO.

One bad pitch!

BLUE JAYS 1 at BRAVES 3
Game One

Toronto	ab	r	h	bi	bb	so	avg.
White cf	4	0	0	0	0	0	.000
RAlomar 2b	4	0	0	0	0	1	.000
Carter 1b	4	1	1	1	0	0	.250
Winfield rf	3	0	1	0	0	0	.333
Maldonado lf	3	0	0	0	0	2	.000
Gruber 3b	3	0	0	0	0	1	.000
Borders c	3	0	2	0	0	0	.667
Lee ss	3	0	0	0	0	0	.000
JaMorris p	2	0	0	0	0	2	.000
Stottlemyre p	0	0	0	0	0	0	—
a-Tabler ph	1	0	0	0	0	0	.000
Wells p	0	0	0	0	0	0	—
Totals	30	1	4	1	0	6	
Atlanta	ab	r	h	bi	bb	so	avg.
Nixon cf	3	0	1	0	1	1	.333
Blauser ss	4	0	0	0	0	2	.000
Belliard ss	0	0	0	0	0	0	—
Pendleton 3b	4	0	0	0	0	0	.000
Justice rf	2	1	0	0	2	1	.000
Bream 1b	3	0	1	0	1	0	.333
Gant lf	3	1	0	0	1	2	.000
Berryhill c	4	1	1	3	0	2	.250
Lemke 2b	3	0	1	0	0	1	.333
Glavine p	2	0	0	0	0	1	.000
Totals	28	3	4	3	6	10	

```
Toronto      000 100 000—1 4 0
Atlanta      000 003 00x—3 4 0
```

a–flied out for Stottlemyre in the 8th.
LOB—Toronto 2, Atlanta 7. HR—Berryhill (1) off Ja-Morris, Carter (1) off Glavine. RBIs—Carter (1), Berryhill 3 (3). SB—Nixon (1), Gant (1). GIDP—Lee.
Runners left in scoring position—Toronto 1 (Lee); Atlanta 4 (Blauser, Justice, Gant 2).
Runners moved up—Pendleton, Gant.
DP—Atlanta 1 (Belliard and Bream).

Toronto	ip	h	r	er	bb	so	np	era
JaMorris L, 0–1	6	4	3	3	5	7	98	4.50
Stottlemyre	1	0	0	0	0	2	13	0.00
Wells	1	0	0	0	1	1	16	0.00
Atlanta	ip	h	r	er	bb	so	np	era
Glavine W, 1–0	9	4	1	1	0	6	128	1.00

WP—JaMorris.
Umpires—Home, Crawford; First, Reilly; Second, West; Third, Morrison; Left, Davidson; Right, Shulock.
T—2:37. A—51,763.

How the runs scored

Jays' fourth: Glavine pitching. Leading off, Carter smashed an 0-1 pitch to left-centre for a home run. Winfield grounded out second to first. Maldonado grounded out short to first. Gruber struck out. **Blue Jays 1, Braves 0.**

Braves' sixth: Morris pitching. Pendleton grounded out second to first. Justice drew a walk. Bream singled to left; Justice to second. Gant forced Bream, short to second. Berryhill lined a 1-2 pitch to right for a home run, also scoring Justice and Gant. Lemke singled to centre. Glavine lined out to centre. **Braves 3, Blue Jays 1.**

Then Jack reaches back and comes up with a great pitch to Ron Gant, which the fleet outfielder taps feebly to short — too feebly, as it turns out. Alomar can't turn the double play after taking a feed from Lee, and Justice goes to third.

But there are two out and Jack can escape just the way he did in the two previous innings — by getting catcher Damon Berryhill, a .228 hitter, any way he wants. When he gets two quick strikes on Berryhill, we know just what he's going to throw: the forkball.

The trouble is, the bottom never falls out. It comes in big and fat and belt-high and Berryhill, a switch hitter who had socked nine of his 10 season homers batting left, loses the ball deep in the right-field seats.

Unfortunately for Morris, there was no room for error in this game. His pitching adversary *wasn't* the Tom Glavine who had won only once since mid-August and posted a 12.27 ERA in two National League playoff losses.

The Glavine who showed up for Game 1 of the World Series was the Cy Young winner from '91, who had also posted 20 wins this season before a cracked rib cramped his style in

August. On this crisp October night, he was all but perfect after the Carter homer. He fanned six, walked none and gave up only three other hits — two to Pat Borders and one to Dave Winfield.

It was clear that Glavine was motivated in this one by all the cruel things people had been saying about him of late. "It was aggravating these past three, four days, having to listen to everything that got said about my pitching in the post-season," he said.

"I guess that's just people's true colors coming out, but it seems like everybody just throws what you did all season long out the window. It's like, 'What have you done for me lately?'

Winfield's flukey second-inning single, which was pounded into the ground and bounced too high for Pendleton to make a play, was the first World Series hit by a Jay. It tied Winfield's previous Series production — he had gone 1 for 22 when he made it to The Show with the Yanks.

Morris joined Joe Bush, Paul Derringer and Grant Jackson as the fourth man to pitch for three different teams in the Series — but none of the others had won for all three teams, and Jack still had a chance to do that.

Morris didn't think his five walks were the main cause of his troubles. "If it's a good pitch, the walks don't matter," Morris said. "When you've got one run to work with, you've got to be careful. Obviously, I want one pitch back.

"Oakland beat us in the first game of the playoffs, too," he added. "Remember, it takes four games to win this."

Anyway, no use crying over spilled splitters. A well-rested David Cone (17-10 on the season, and the major league strikeout leader with 288) was all set to face John Smoltz (15-12 and 215 strikeouts) in Game 2. Smoltz had been Atlanta's ace of late, but he would be going with only three days' rest. We all knew what that could mean.

MIKE SLAUGHTER

CY YOUNG FORM IS DISPLAYED BY BRAVES' STARTER TOM GLAVINE
WHO GAVE UP ONLY FOUR HITS AND WALKED NO ONE IN GAME 1.

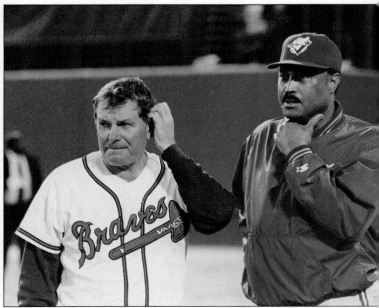

MIKE SLAUGHTER

BASEBALL'S A PUZZLE, FORMER JAYS MANAGER BOBBY COX AND
PRESENT MANAGER CITO GASTON AGREE BEFORE SERIES STARTS.

SPRAGUE COMES UP WITH A STROKE OF GENIUS

GAME 2

Jays 5 at Braves 4

We all have *those* days, don't we?

Days when the car won't start, the boss ticks you off and you spill ketchup on your shirt.

When *everything* seems to go wrong, what can you do?

Keep swinging, of course. Have faith and hope something nice will happen.

Because bad days and nights *can* have beautiful endings — as Ed Sprague and the Blue Jays would prove at 15 minutes to midnight this unforgettable Sunday in Atlanta.

It looked like a rough night for Canada's team right from the start, didn't it, as Toronto rocker Tom ("Life is a Highway") Cochrane struggled through a pathetic, weak-voiced rendition of "O Canada."

Now, here comes the U.S. Marine color guard and . . . *Holy smoke!* Can you believe it? They've got the Canadian flag . . . NWOD 3DISPU!

Within minutes, protests are pouring into media centres across Canada. But early in the game, some of us are wondering if that misguided Marine hadn't been right. Isn't an inverted flag the universal signal of distress?

On the mound, while Atlanta ace John Smoltz is striking out five of the first six Jays, David Cone is throwing hard but missing the strike zone And his catcher and shortstop aren't helping much.

In the second inning, slow-footed Dave Justice easily steals second on Pat Borders' bad throw. Then Manuel Lee compounds the problem with an ill-advised attempt to nail Justice at third on a routine grounder from Jeff Blauser.

When Borders fails to block a Cone pitch in the dirt, Justice rumbles in from third and the Braves have drawn first blood.

It gets worse. Roberto Alomar, who had combined with Devon White to make the top of the order 0 for 11 in the Series, draws a walk to lead off the fourth, moves to second on a wild pitch and takes third on a Dave Winfield groundout.

On the first pitch to John Olerud, the ball gets away from Braves catcher Damon Berryhill and bounces 30 feet to the right. Here comes Alomar. Berryhill retrieves the ball and shovels it to Smoltz, who is covering the plate. Alomar slides! He is safe!

Except in the eyes of home plate umpire Mike Reilly, who rules him *OUT!*

As many replays would show, Robbie beat the tag. One of those nights.

Minutes later, a Mark Lemke single scores Sid Bream to make it 2-0 Atlanta. The tomahawk-chopping crowd of 51,763 is in full chant.

In the fifth, the Jays are on a treadmill of futility when Olerud and Kelly Gruber make quick outs. Dramatic action is called for — so Cito Gaston trots out to complain about the white bandage on Smoltz's forearm.

JEFF GOODE

INTERNATIONAL INCIDENT WAS CREATED IN GAME 2 WHEN THE MARINE COLOR GUARD PARADED THE CANADIAN FLAG UPSIDE DOWN.

79

Well, that did the trick. After changing bandages, the hitherto indomitable Smoltz promptly walks Borders and yields a single to Lee, setting the stage for one of the most entertaining moments of the Series.

Cone, who'd already stroked the Jays' first hit, is due up. American League pitchers are still only 3 for 89 in post-season play, but Cito lets him hit.

And Cone comes through! Lining a single to drive in Borders. When White's infield chopper scores Lee, we're tied.

But the happy times don't last. Singles by Deion Sanders and Justice, plus a walk to Terry Pendleton and a throwing error by Borders, produce a run and chase Cone. David Wells yields a sacrifice fly to Brian Hunter and it's 4-2.

The Jays finally dispatch Smoltz in the eighth via an Alomar double, and singles by Joe Carter and Winfield. But Gruber whiffs (0 for 22 at this point) against Jeff Reardon and it's 4-3 with just one more chance.

With one out in the ninth, here comes Derek Bell to pinch hit for Lee. He is caught looking at a third strike — except that Reilly calls it a ball. Bell is on with a walk, as backup catcher Sprague comes to the plate to hit for pitcher Duane Ward.

Backup catcher — that should have been the tipoff, shouldn't it, considering Francisco Cabrera's heroics to win the NL pennant four days earlier and Berryhill's three-run shot the night before?

The first pitch from Reardon is a waist-high batting practice fastball. POW! Gone.

Suddenly, shockingly, the Jays have a 5-4 lead. The Tomahawk Chop chant has died.

In the bottom of the ninth, Sprague's wife, Olympic gold medal synchro swimmer Kristen Babb-Sprague, is waving a big, blue, foam rubber J. On the other side of the field, Jane Fonda has her hands clasped as if in prayer.

On the mound, Tom Henke has troubles of his own: the tying run on second (Ron Gant), the winning run on first (Sanders) and the league's leading clutch hitter, with a .387 average with men in scoring position, at the plate (Pendleton).

Heeeere's the pitch! POP-UP! Gruber's got it.

On to the SkyDome, where the flags are flying upright.

MIKE SLAUGHTER

COLIN McCONNELL

GETTING HIS REWARD FROM WIFE KRISTEN IS ED SPRAGUE AFTER DRAMATIC 9TH-INNING HOME RUN.

APOPLECTIC ALOMAR GOES AFTER MIKE REILLY AFTER THE UMP BLEW A CALL ON THE SLIDING JAY AT HOME PLATE.

MIKE SLAUGHTER

UNLIKEY HEROES, DEREK BELL AND SPRAGUE, CELEBRATE AT THE PLATE AFTER THE BIG TWO-RUN BLAST.

81

Rookie rocks em!

BLUE JAYS 5 at BRAVES 4
Game Two

Toronto	ab	r	h	bi	bb	so	avg.
White cf	5	0	1	1	0	1	.111
RAlomar 2b	4	1	1	0	1	1	.286
Carter lf	3	0	1	0	1	1	.286
Winfield rf	4	0	1	1	0	0	.000
Olerud 1b	4	0	0	0	0	3	.000
Gruber 3b	3	1	1	0	1	0	.500
Borders c	3	1	1	0	1	0	.167
Lee ss	0	1	0	0	1	0	—
c-DBell ph	0	0	0	0	1	0	—
Griffin ss	2	0	2	1	0	0	1.000
Cone p	2	0	0	0	0	1	.000
Wells p	0	0	0	0	0	0	—
b-Maldndo ph	1	0	0	0	0	1	.000
Stottlemyre p	0	0	0	0	0	0	—
DWard p	1	1	1	2	0	0	1.000
d-Sprague ph	0	0	0	0	0	0	—
Henke p	0	0	0	0	0	0	—
Totals	34	5	9	5	4	9	
Atlanta	ab	r	h	bi	bb	so	avg.
Nixon cf	5	0	0	0	0	1	.125
DSanders lf	3	1	1	0	2	0	.333
Pendleton 3b	4	1	1	0	2	0	.125
Justice rf	3	1	1	1	1	0	.200
Bream 1b	1	0	0	1	2	0	.250
a-Hunter ph-1b	1	0	0	1	0	0	.000
Blauser ss	3	0	1	0	1	1	.143
Belliard ss	0	0	0	0	0	0	—
Berryhill c	3	0	0	0	1	2	.143
Lemke 2b	4	0	1	1	0	0	.286
Smoltz p	3	0	0	0	0	2	.000
Stanton p	0	0	0	0	0	0	—
Reardon p	0	0	0	0	0	0	—
e-LSmith ph	0	0	0	0	0	0	.000
1-Gant pr	0	0	0	0	0	0	—
Totals	30	4	5	3	7	6	

Toronto	000 020 012—5	9 2
Atlanta	010 120 000—4	5 1

a—hit sacrifice fly for Bream in the 5th. b—struck out for Wells in the 7th. c—walked for Lee in the 9th. d—homered for D.Ward in the 9th. e—was hit by pitch for Reardon in the 9th.

1—ran for L.Smith in the 9th.

E—Borders (1), Lee (1), Bream (1). LOB—Toronto 6, Atlanta 8. 2B—RAlomar (1), Borders (1). HR—Sprague (1) off Reardon. RBIs—White (1), Winfield (1), Cone (1), Sprague 2 (2), Justice (1), Hunter (1), Lemke (1). SB—DSanders 2 (2), Justice (1), Blauser (1), Gant (2). SF—Hunter. GIDP—Lemke, Smoltz.

Toronto	ip	h	r	er	bb	so	np
Cone	4 1/3	5	4	3	5	2	94
Wells	1 2/3	0	0	0	1	2	18
Stottlemyre	1	0	0	0	0	0	8
DWard W,1-0	1	0	0	0	0	2	15
Henke S,1	1	0	0	1	0	2	20
Atlanta	ip	h	r	er	bb	so	np
Smoltz	7 1/3	8	3	2	3	8	121
Stanton	1/3	0	0	0	0	1	1
Reardon L,0-1	1 1/3	1	2	2	1	1	20

How the runs scored

Braves second: Justice walked. Bream flied out to centre. With one out, Justice stole second. Blauser grounded to short and was safe at first, Justice safe at third, when Lee's throw to third hit Justice in the back. Cone's wild pitch allowed Justice to score. **Braves 1, Jays 0.**

Braves fourth: Bream led off with a walk. With Bream running, Blauser lined a single to right that sent Bream to third. Lemke singled to right, Bream scoring. **Braves 2, Jays 0.**

Jays fifth: Smoltz pitching. Olerud flew out to right. Gruber grounded out to third. Borders walked. Lee singled to right, Borders to second. Cone singled to centre, Borders scored. White's infield single to second base scored Lee. **Braves 2, Jays 2.**

Braves fifth: Sanders singled to right, stole second, and went to third on Borders' throwing error. Pendleton walked. Justice singled to right, scoring Sanders, Pendleton to third. Wells replaced Stottlemyre. Hunter hit a sacrifice fly to right, scoring Pendleton. **Braves 4, Jays 2.**

Jays eighth: After White led off with a fly ball out to centre, Alomar doubled into the left field corner and took third on Carter's single up the middle. Winfield singled to right, scoring Alomar. **Braves 4, Jays 3.**

Jays ninth: Reardon pitching. Borders led off with a fly ball out to centre. Bell, pinch-hitting for Lee, walked. Sprague, pinch-hitting for Ward, smacked a home run to left. **Blue Jays 5, Braves 4.**

HOW SWEET IT IS — CANDY STICKS IT TO BRAVES

GAME 3

Braves 2 at Jays 3

Just when you think you've seen the best baseball game of your life, along comes another one that's even better.

Game 3 of the World Series, for sure — the one where the Blue Jays beat the National Leaguers at their own game.

The first Series contest ever played in Canada was packed with powerful memories, including the best catch most of the 51,813 at the SkyDome had ever witnessed. But nothing quite matched the bottom of the ninth for the kind of excitement that makes heart doctors rich.

That final inning started, as most good Blue Jay things do, with Robbie Alomar. Leading off with the score tied at two, the Jays' MVP candidate is in the worst slump of his young career: 1 for 11 in the Series, and a Steve Avery strikeout victim twice in the game.

This time, he drills a single up the middle to drive Avery to the showers. His hit immediately elevates the game to one of those chess-master contests that Bobby Cox and National League fans love so well: "You give me a lefthanded hitter and I'll counter with a lefthanded pitcher; you change back and I'll change back, until the only one left on the bench is the trainer."

Bobby, however, is managing blindly from the runway to the visitors dressing room, having been tossed in the top of the inning for hurling a helmet on to the field in disgust after manoeuvring his team into a rally-killing double play. With trusted third base coach Jimy Williams — like Cox, a one-time Jays manager — carrying out the orders, Bobby pulls his power-pitching starter mostly because his high leg kick would make it too easy for Alomar to steal.

He goes to righthanded reliever Mark Wohlers, who throws even harder than Avery does (clocked at 100 m.p.h. in the playoffs). The Braves try a pitchout, with catcher Damon Berryhill snapping a strike to first that might have nailed almost anyone — but not Alomar. He gets back with that patented dive to the outfield side of the bag.

Then, on a 2-and-0 count to Joe Carter, Alomar steals after

RICHARD LAUTENS

ONLY SUPERMAN AND DEVON WHITE MAKE CATCHES LIKE THIS AND SUPERMAN ISN'T PLAYING ANYMORE — IT SNUFFED OUT A 4TH INNING RALLY IN GAME THREE.

RICHARD LAUTENS

ALL FLAGS WERE FLYING RIGHT SIDE UP THIS NIGHT-AS GUZMAN FANNED SEVEN AND THE JAYS WON IT IN THE NINTH.

MIKE SLAUGHTER

Rally time!

BRAVES 2 at BLUE JAYS 3
Game Three

Atlanta	ab	r	h	bi	bb	so	avg.
Nixon cf	4	1	0	0	0	0	.083
DSanders lf	4	1	3	0	0	0	.571
Pendleton 3b	4	0	2	0	0	0	.250
Justice rf	3	0	1	1	1	1	.250
LSmith dh	4	0	1	1	0	2	.250
Bream 1b	4	0	2	0	0	0	.375
1-Hunter pr-1b	0	0	0	0	0	0	.000
Blauser ss	4	0	0	0	0	3	.091
Berryhill c	4	0	0	0	0	3	.091
Lemke 2b	3	0	0	0	0	0	.200
Totals	34	2	9	2	1	9	
Toronto	ab	r	h	bi	bb	so	avg.
White cf	4	0	0	0	0	2	.077
RAlomar 2b	4	1	1	0	0	2	.167
Carter rf	3	1	1	1	1	0	.300
Winfield dh	3	0	1	0	0	1	.300
Olerud 1b	3	0	0	0	0	2	.000
a-Sprague ph	0	0	0	0	1	0	1.000
Maldonado lf	4	0	1	1	0	1	.125
Gruber 3b	2	1	1	1	1	0	.111
Borders c	3	0	1	0	0	1	.444
Lee ss	3	0	0	0	0	0	.111
Totals	29	3	6	3	3	9	

Atlanta	000	001	010—2	9	0	
Toronto	000	100	011—3	6	1	

One out when winning run scored.
a—was intentionally walked for Olerud in the 9th.
1-ran for Bream in the 9th.
E—Gruber (1). LOB—Atlanta 6, Toronto 5. 2B—DSanders (1). HR—Carter (2) off Avery, Gruber (1) off Avery. RBIs—Justice (2), LSmith (1), Carter (2), Maldonado (1), Gruber (1). SB—Nixon (2), DSanders (3), RAlomar (1), Gruber (1). CS—Hunter (1). S—Winfield. GIDP—Maldonado.
Runners left in scoring position—Atlanta 3 (Justice, LSmith, Bream); Toronto 2 (White, Lee).
Runners moved up—Pendleton 2, Lee.
DP—Atlanta 1 (Pendleton, Lemke and Bream); Toronto 2 (White and Lee), (Borders and Lee).

Atlanta	ip	h	r	er	bb	so	np	era
Avery L, 0–1	8	5	3	3	1	9	115	3.38
Wohlers	⅓	0	0	0	1	0	4	0.00
Stanton	0	0	0	0	1	0	0	0.00
Reardon	0	1	0	0	0	0	3	13.50
Toronto	ip	h	r	er	bb	so	np	era
JuGuzman	8	8	2	1	1	7	112	1.12
DWard W, 2–0	1	1	0	0	0	2	12	0.00

How the runs scored

Jays fourth: Avery pitching. Alomar grounded to third for the first out. Carter delivered the first pitch into the left field bleachers, a 405-foot shot and his second of the World Series. Winfield popped to second. Olerud grounded out to the pitcher. **1 run, 1 hit, 0 errors, 0 left on base. Jays 1, Braves 0.**

Braves sixth: Guzman pitching. Nixon led off with a ground ball out to second. Sanders doubled to right for his third consecutive hit of the game. Pendleton hit an infield single to Lee, who threw to third too late to get Sanders. Justice singled to right, scoring Sanders and putting Pendleton at second. Smith lined out to right. Bream grounded out to first. **1 run, 3 hits, 0 errors, 2 left on base. Jays 1, Braves 1.**

Braves eighth: Nixon reached first on a hard-hit ball off Gruber's glove at third that was ruled an error. Nixon stole second. Sanders popped out to short. Pendleton grounded to second and was out, Alomar to Olerud, Nixon to third. Justice was walked intentionally. Smith singled to left, scoring Nixon, Justice out trying to reach third on the play. **1 run, 1 hit, 1 error, 0 left on base. Braves 2, Jays 1.**

Jays eighth: Gruber led off with a 362-foot home run just inside the left-field foul pole on a 3-2 pitch. Borders flied out to deep centre. **1 run, 1 hit, 0 errors, 0 left on base. Braves 2, Jays 2.**

Jays ninth: Alomar led off with a single up the middle. Wohlers replaced Avery. Alomar stole second, his first stolen base of the Series. Carter was intentionally walked. Winfield sacrifice bunted, Alomar to third, Carter to second. Stanton replaced Wohlers. Sprague, in to pinch-hit for Olerud, was intentionally walked. Reardon replaced Stanton. Maldonado singled to centre. **1 run, 2 hits, 0 errors, 3 left on base. Jays 3, Braves 2.**

83

getting such a big jump that even John Olerud could have made it. Well, maybe not. The Braves decide it might be prudent to intentionally walk Carter, who had already drilled a home run deep to left.

Up steps Dave Winfield in a situation that screams for a sacrifice. But the 41-year-old slugger has bunted only once this year. He lays it down too hard and too deep to the first base side, but it catches everyone napping. They manage to nail him at first, but Alomar and Carter advance easily.

In comes Mike Stanton, the almost unhittable lefty, to pitch to Olerud. But Cito Gaston, who is getting to like this chess stuff, counters with Ed Sprague, the righthanded-hitting backup catcher whose dramatic ninth-inning homer had tied the Series in Atlanta.

Now I gotcha, Bobby figures. He orders a walk to Sprague to load the bases and goes back to his bullpen for righthanded closer Jeff Reardon, the man Sprague had victimized two nights earlier, to pitch to Candy Maldonado.

Righty against righty. The bases loaded. The outfield in. The guy with the most saves in the history of baseball on the mound. St. John Ambulance attendants nervously eyeing red-faced fans.

The Candy Man, odd man out for the Jays when the season started, has had a fine year but is having a nightmare of a night at the plate, hitting into a double play, fanning and lofting an easy fly to centre. And he's 2 for 13 lifetime against Reardon.

Two quick strikes and Reardon is ready to blow him away.

BOOS ENDED RIGHT HERE FOR KELLY GRUBER, SEEN
CIRCLING THE BASES AFTER HIS 8TH INNING, GAME-TYING HOMER.

Candy looks strangely uncomfortable, about as confident as a guy who works in a chocolate factory going for a dental check-up. But incredibly, the next pitch hangs out where nobody has any business putting an 0-and-2 pitch, even when the bases aren't loaded.

Candy drives it over centre fielder Otis Nixon's head and Alomar trots in with the winning run. It's celebration time again!

And what a bunch of things there were to celebrate. THE CATCH, for starters. When this Series is re-lived in years to come, it will simply be known as The Catch. Everyone will know which one you mean.

It came in the top of the fourth, with pitcher Juan Guzman in a pack of trouble. Deion Sanders is on second and Terry Pendleton on first with no one out. Cleanup man David Justice catches hold of a high, hard one and drives it deep to centre. Might be a homer; sure to drive in at least two runs.

But there's Devon White, not gliding but sprinting for the fence, right at the 400-foot mark. He goes up, up and away, grabbing the ball just as he crashes into the wall. Then he lands like an acrobat and fires it back to the infield, where the Braves are busy self-destructing.

Pendleton, who knows a sure hit when he sees one, has raced past Olerud, Alomar and, incredibly, right by Sanders, who hesitates because of Devo's reputation for making the impossible happen and the improbable look easy.

Not realizing Pendleton is automatically out for passing Sanders, the Jays throw to first to double him up, then fire to Kelly Gruber, who has Sanders in a rundown — chasing, chasing, then diving and apparently clipping him on the heel for the second triple play in Series history. Except that umpire Bob Davidson calls the Neon man safe. TV and news photos have some incriminating shots, but nothing conclusive enough to send Davidson to prison. But later, Davidson sees TV clips of the play and admits he probably blew it.

Quite a night for Gruber. He had made the only error of the game, leading to a run by Nixon that gave the Braves a 2-1 lead. In the third, he set a record for post-season incompetence at the plate by going hitless in 23 straight at-bats.

Still, up he comes in the eighth, just as the dream was starting to die and people weren't standing up any more for every pitch. On a 3-and-2 count, he catches the same kind of hard, outside pitch that Avery gave Carter and pulls it into the left-field stands to tie the score.

"Right now, I'm a hero," Gruber mused after the game. "I'd be pretty surprised to hear any boos tomorrow . . . before my first at-bat."

Guzman was a little short of wonderful in this one, giving up one earned run, eight hits and striking out seven before departing after the eighth. Duane Ward came in to take care of the ninth and earn his second Series win.

Avery, who had a mediocre season, was superb, giving up only five hits and fanning nine. Unfortunately for him, two of those hits were homers and he didn't have Ward in his bullpen. So, he was tagged with the loss.

The SkyDome handled the flag incident with such class that those who showed up with plans to stay seated for the U.S. anthem, and other bits of talk-show-instigated nonsense, were left cold. The Marines returned to proudly parade the Canadian flag right side up. And that's the way the whole night ended.

KEY IS ALL CLASS IN KEY SERIES WIN

COLIN McCONNELL

GAME 4

Braves 1 at Jays 2

In his finest moment, he doesn't swagger, for that is not his way.

As the rapturous SkyDome ovation rolls over him, he merely tips his cap in a gesture that says: Thank you.

To which millions of us would reply: Thank *you,* Jimmy Key.

Thank you for showing us the art of pitching at its best. Thank you for proving once again that loyalty, determination and character still have their rewards.

And thank you for bringing the Blue Jays to the threshold of a 3-1 lead in this historic World Series.

Mind you, as the Thinking Fan's Pitcher departs the mound with two out in the top of the eighth inning, there's still work to be done. The Braves have just scored, and the tying run is on base.

Remember? When the inning began, the Jays led 2-0 and Key had retired 20 of Atlanta's last 21 batters. But Ron Gant breaks a personal 0-for-16 famine with a double down the left-field line past a diving Kelly Gruber.

When Brian Hunter follows with a perfect bunt single, the Braves have runners at first and third, nobody out. Next up is Damon Berryhill.

Since he stroked that three-run homer to win Game 1 in Atlanta, the Braves catcher had gone 0 for 12 with eight strikeouts. Now, if he can steer a ball through the infield, or even tap a grounder on the right side, he can be a hero again.

But Berryhill has other ideas. Apparently missing a hit-and-run sign, he decides to *bunt* — and pops it up to Pat

AFTER A MASTERFUL, FIVE-HIT PERFORMANCE, JIMMY KEY QUIETLY DOFFS HIS CAP TO THE CROWD AS HE TURNS THE GAME OVER TO THE BULLPEN IN THE 7TH.

DICK LOEK

Borders in foul territory. Whew! Thank you, Damon!

The next hitter, second baseman Mark Lemke, takes a more conventional approach — lining a shot off the mound in front of Key. Here comes the run, and here comes Gruber — barehanding the ball behind the mound and firing a bullet to John Olerud to nail Lemke by a step. Outstanding!

Now, with switch-hitting Otis Nixon due up, it's time for Key to turn the ball over to Duane Ward and make his exit to a standing ovation.

Question: How many of those 52,090 adoring fans had such warm feelings two hours earlier, when Nixon and Jeff Blauser started the game with back-to-back, line-drive singles?

Fortunately, Key was able to pick Nixon off first and escape without damage. But when big boppers Terry Pendleton and Dave Justice followed with laser shots right at Jay gloves, many had the feeling Key was living on borrowed time.

Time. That was the problem. Sixteen days between starts for a pitcher who relies on finesse. But after dropping Key from the rotation in the Oakland series, Cito wanted to give his classy lefty a chance. There's a word for that: loyalty.

Then, about the middle of the third inning, it becomes clear that things have changed. Key has retired six straight after Blauser's hit. He has his rhythm and he is throwing strikes. He will fan six and walk none in the fastest Series game in seven years (two hours, 21 minutes).

His opponent, Tom Glavine, is also going well. But American League umpire Dan Morrison isn't giving him those just-off-the-plate called strikes he'd received from National Leaguer Jerry Crawford in his impressive Game 1 victory.

In the third, Borders gets just enough of a 1-and-1 Glavine offering to clear the fence beside the left-field foul pole. It's Borders' first homer off a lefty all year, and the Jays lead 1-0.

Four innings later, Devon White delivers his third hit of the night, a two-out single that brings Gruber home in a jarring head-first slide that bloodies his chin and leaves him woozy.

As Key departs with a one-run lead, we're wondering: Can the Jays hang on? More to the point: Can Borders hang on?

Once again, we see a familiar chilling sight: Ward strikes out Nixon with a hellacious sinker. But the ball gets by Borders — allowing Nixon to reach first, and moving Hunter all the way to third.

With the tying run so close, Braves manager Bobby Cox renders the kind of decision that makes baseball such a second-guesser's delight.

With two potent lefthanded hitters (Sid Bream and Deion Sanders) fingering bats on the bench, Cox allows the righthanded Blauser (4 for 34 in the post-season) to hit against the righthanded Ward.

The result: a grounder to Olerud, and the Braves are gone.

Thirteen minutes later, Tom Henke has dispatched Pendleton, Lonnie Smith and Justice on just 11 pitches and it's over.

Now the Braves must beat Jack Morris, David Cone and Juan Guzman to win the Series.

DICK LOEK

FRONT-ROW FIELDERS HAD FUN GOING AFTER A LOOSE BALL BEFORE GAME 4. BUT IN GAME 5 A FAN GOT THROWN OUT FOR INTERFERING WITH THE FIRST HIT, A DOUBLE BY OTIS NIXON.

JEFF GOODE

DICK LOEK

SLIDING ACROSS WITH THE GAME-WINNING RUN, KELLY GRUBER EMERGED
LOOKING LIKE THE LOSER IN A STREET BRAWL.

Gruber a hit!

BRAVES 1 at BLUE JAYS 2
Game Four

Atlanta	ab	r	h	bi	bb	so	avg.
Nixon cf	4	0	2	0	0	1	.188
Blauser ss	4	0	1	0	0	1	.133
Pendleton 3b	4	0	0	0	0	1	.188
LSmith dh	4	0	0	0	0	1	.125
Justice rf	4	0	0	0	0	1	.167
Gant lf	3	1	1	0	0	0	.167
Hunter 1b	3	0	1	0	0	1	.250
Berryhill c	3	0	0	0	0	1	.071
Lemke 2b	3	0	0	1	0	1	.154
Totals	32	1	5	1	0	8	
Toronto	ab	r	h	bi	bb	so	avg.
White cf	4	0	3	1	0	0	.235
RAlomar 2b	3	0	0	0	1	0	.133
Carter rf	3	0	0	0	1	0	.231
Winfield dh	3	0	0	0	1	0	.231
Olerud 1b	3	0	2	0	0	1	.200
Maldonado lf	3	0	0	0	0	1	.091
Gruber 3b	2	1	0	0	1	0	.091
Borders c	3	1	1	1	0	0	.417
Lee ss	3	0	0	0	0	0	.083
Totals	27	2	6	2	4	2	

Atlanta	000	000	010—1	5	0		
Toronto	001	000	10x—2	6	0		

LOB—Atlanta 4, Toronto 5. 2B—Gant (1), White (1).
HR—Borders (1) off Glavine. RBIs—Lemke (2), White
(2), Borders (1). SB—Nixon (3), Blauser (2), RAlomar
(2). GIDP—Gruber.
    Runners left in scoring position—Atlanta 3 (Blauser
2, LSmith); Toronto 3 (Winfield, Maldonado, Gruber).
Runners moved up—Lemke, Carter, Lee.
    DP—Atlanta 2 (Blauser and Lemke), (Blauser,
Lemke and Hunter).

Atlanta	ip	h	r	er	bb	so	np	era
Glavine L, 1–1	8	6	2	2	4	2	114	1.59
Toronto	ip	h	r	er	bb	so	np	era
Key W, 1–0	7 ⅔	5	1	1	0	6	91	1.17
DWard	⅓	0	0	0	0	1	8	0.00
Henke S, 2	1	0	0	0	1	1	11	0.00

    Inherited runners–scored—DWard 1–0.
WP—DWard.
    Umpires—Home, Morrison; First, Davidson; Sec-
ond, Shulock; Third, Crawford; Left, Reilly; Right,
West.
    T–2:21. A—52,090.

How the runs scored

Jays' third: Glavine pitching. Borders,
leading off, hit a 1-1 pitch off the fair pole
in left for his first homer. Lee grounded
out, second to first. White doubled to
right. Alomar walked. Carter lined into a
double play, to short and short to second
on White. **1 run, 2 hits, 0 errors, 1 left on
base. Blue Jays 1, Braves 0.**
    Jays' seventh: Gruber, leading off,
drew a walk. Borders flew out to centre.
Lee grounded out, pitcher to first, advancing Gruber to third. White singled to left,
driving in Gruber; White out trying to advance, left fielder to third, to second, to
first. **1 run, 1 hit, 0 errors, 1 left on base.
Blue Jays 2, Braves 0.**
    Braves' eighth: Key pitching. Gant led
off with a double to left. Hunter beat out a
bunt single to third, advancing Gant to
third. Berryhill popped out to the catcher.
Lemke grounded out, pitcher to third to
first, driving in Gant. Ward replaced Key.
Nixon struck out, but reached first on
Ward's wild pitch; Hunter to third. Blauser
grounded out to first. **1 runs, 2 hits, 0
errors, 2 left on base. Blue Jays 2,
Braves 1.**

87

SERIES GRAND SLAMMED BACK TO DIXIE

GAME 5

Braves 7 at Jays 2

In Game 5 of the World Series, the Jays' $5 million man wasn't worth five cents. And Jack Morris was the first to admit it.

"The Atlanta Braves have won two games and I've pitched both of them," he said after the 7-2 shellacking that sent the Series back to Atlanta. "They're in trouble . . . they're in serious trouble, because I don't pitch again."

All year long, Morris had proven that the right kind of pitcher can give up four runs a game and still be a big winner. In the playoffs and World Series, he proved just as conclusively that a pitcher who gives up twice that many runs is an albatross around his team's neck.

His ERA was 8.44 in the Series and 8.26 in the whole postseason, in which he had lost three games, won none and messed up another. Yet, it was post-season wins they were looking for when members of the Jays braintrust shelled out the most money they had ever paid a player, as a Christmas present to Morris last December. At the time, however, they didn't realize they were getting a pitcher who had become so mellow that he was actually civil to sportswriters — at least most of them.

Fans who lustily booed his departure after the fifth-inning debacle at the SkyDome, however, might have had short memories (or big bets on the Jays). During the season, Black

Jack was 21-6 and the only starter manager Cito Gaston could depend on in the dog days of August, when the birds of Baltimore closed to within half a game. Without him, the Jays could have traded their bats and gloves for fishing rods and golf clubs on Oct. 4.

"Did I leave Jack in too long?" Cito asked, in answer to a reporter's question that wasn't put quite so politely. "I guess the results show that I did, but I believe in Jack a lot."

Cito, hands-down winner of the most loyal manager in the majors award (for which there is no trophy), even said he thought the crowd was booing *him*, not Black Jack. But anyone within earshot of fulminating fans, in every section of the park, knew the blame was meant to be shared equally — preferably by firing squad.

That fifth inning might have been the worst of the 3,381 that Morris has pitched since he made his big league debut, at the same time as the original Blue Jays in 1977.

With the score tied at two, it starts out like kid's play as Morris fans catcher Damon Berryhill and gets second baseman Mark Lemke to bounce to Robbie Alomar. But leadoff hitter Otis Nixon slashes a double past Kelly Gruber, and promptly steals his fifth base of the Series. Deion Sanders drives him in with a single to shallow centre to give the Braves a 3-2 lead, then takes third on a double by Terry Pendleton, which is touched by a fan.

David Justice, who had already homered off Morris, is intentionally walked to get at long-in-the-tooth Lonnie Smith, who is almost as old as the Jays' 37-year-old starter.

In Atlanta, fans were booing Braves manager Bobby Cox for continuing to use Smith, 1 for 10 as he stands in against Morris. But Cox says Smith is the toughest player he has ever

COLIN McCONNELL

DUGOUT DEPRESSION. JACK MORRIS DRIES OFF WITH A TOWEL AS HIS MATES LET THE RAMIFICATION OF HIS 5TH-INNING DISASTER SINK IN.

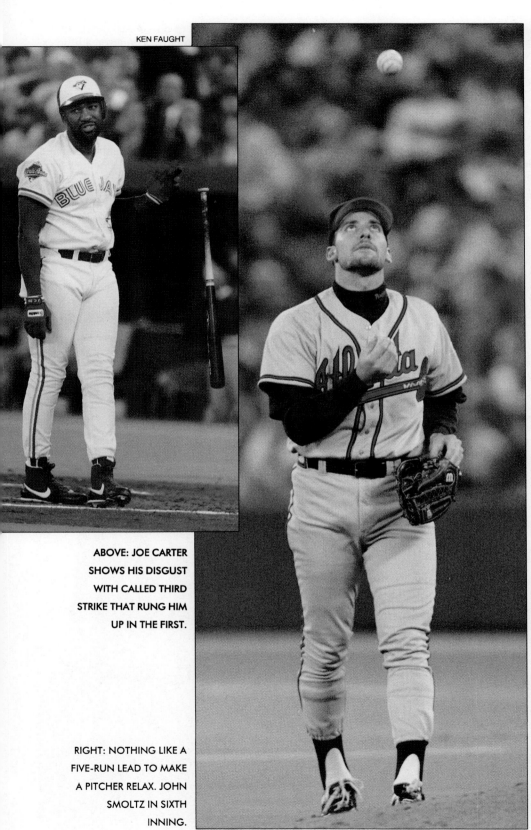

KEN FAUGHT

ABOVE: JOE CARTER SHOWS HIS DISGUST WITH CALLED THIRD STRIKE THAT RUNG HIM UP IN THE FIRST.

RIGHT: NOTHING LIKE A FIVE-RUN LEAD TO MAKE A PITCHER RELAX. JOHN SMOLTZ IN SIXTH INNING.

KEN FAUGHT

Morris mauled!

BRAVES 7 at BLUE JAYS 2
Game Five

Atlanta	ab	r	h	bi	bb	so	avg.
Nixon cf	5	2	3	0	0	0	.286
DSanders lf	5	1	2	1	0	1	.500
Pendleton 3b	5	1	2	1	0	1	.238
Justice rf	3	2	1	1	1	1	.200
LSmith dh	4	1	1	4	0	1	.167
Bream 1b	4	0	0	0	0	0	.250
Blauser ss	4	0	1	0	0	1	.158
Belliard ss	0	0	0	0	0	0	—
Berryhill c	4	0	1	0	0	2	.111
Lemke 2b	4	0	2	0	0	0	.235
Totals	**38**	**7**	**13**	**7**	**1**	**7**	
Toronto	ab	r	h	bi	bb	so	avg.
White cf	4	0	0	0	0	2	.190
RAlomar 2b	3	0	0	1	0	0	.111
Carter rf	4	0	1	0	0	1	.235
Winfield dh	4	0	1	0	0	1	.235
Olerud 1b	3	2	2	0	0	0	.308
a-Sprague ph-1b	1	0	0	0	0	0	.500
Maldonado lf	2	0	0	0	2	0	.077
Gruber 3b	4	0	0	0	0	1	.067
Borders c	4	0	2	2	0	0	.438
Lee ss	3	0	0	0	1	0	.067
Totals	**32**	**2**	**6**	**2**	**4**	**5**	
Atlanta	100	150	000—7	13	0		
Toronto	010	100	000—2	6	0		

a—flied out for Olerud in the 8th.

LOB—Atlanta 5, Toronto 7. 2B—Nixon (1), Pendleton 2 (2), Borders (2). HR—Justice (1) off JaMorris, LSmith (1) off JaMorris. RBIs—DSanders (1), Pendleton (1), Justice (3), LSmith 4 (5), Borders 2 (3). SB—Nixon 2 (5). CS—Blauser (1). GIDP—RAlomar.
Runners left in scoring position—Atlanta 2 (Pendleton, LSmith); Toronto 4 (White, Maldonado, Lee 2).
Runners moved up—Nixon, DSanders, Sprague, Lee.
DP—Atlanta 1 (Lemke, Blauser and Bream); Toronto 1 (Maldonado and Borders).

Atlanta	ip	h	r	er	bb	so	np	era
Smoltz W, 1–0	6	5	2	2	4	4	114	2.70
Stanton S, 1	3	1	0	0	0	1	41	0.00
Toronto	ip	h	r	er	bb	so	np	era
JaMorris L, 0–2	4 ⅔	9	7	7	1	5	79	8.44
Wells	1 ⅓	1	0	0	0	0	19	0.00
Timlin	1	0	0	0	0	0	9	0.00
Eichhorn	1	0	0	0	0	1	14	0.00
Stottlemyre	1	3	0	0	1	1	17	0.00

Smoltz pitched to 1 batter in the 7th.
Inherited runners-scored—Stanton 1–0.
IBB—off JaMorris (Justice) 1.
Umpires—Home, Davidson; First, Shulock; Second, Crawford; Third, Reilly; Left, West; Right, Morrison. T—3:05. A—52,268.

How the runs scored

Braves' first: Morris pitching. Nixon hit a ground-rule double into the left-field seats on the first pitch. After Sanders struck out, Nixon stole third, then scored on Pendleton's double to right. Justice fanned and Smith flied out to left. **1 run, 2 hits, 0 errors, 1 left on base. Braves 1, Blue Jays 0.**

Jays' second: Smoltz pitching. Winfield flied to centre and Olerud singled. Maldonado walked. After Gruber struck out, Borders doubled to left, scoring Olerud, Maldonado to third. Lee lined to third. **1 run, 2 hits, 0 errors, 2 left on base. Blue Jays 1, Braves 1.**

Braves' fourth: Justice opened with a homer to right. Smith and Bream flied out. Blauser singled to left, then was caught stealing, Borders to Lee. **1 runs, 2 hits, 0 errors, 0 left on base. Braves 2, Blue Jays 1.**

Jays' fourth: Olerud opened with a single to right and Maldonado walked. Gruber flied out at the fence in left. Borders singled through the box to score Olerud, Maldonado to third. Lee reached on a fielder's choice that forced Maldonado at third. White struck out. **Blue Jays 2, Braves 2.**

Braves' fifth: Berryhill fanned and Lemke bounced to second. Nixon singled, stole second and scored on Sanders' single to centre. Pendleton hit a ground-rule double to right and Sanders was forced to stay at third. Justice was walked intentionally to load the bases. Smith homered into the Atlanta bullpen, the 16th grandslam in Series history. Wells came in to pitch for Morris and Bream flied to left. **5 runs, 4 hits, 0 errors, 0 left on base. Braves 7, Blue Jays 2.**

managed. Also, the sacks are drunk and Smith has clubbed three grand slams in his career.

Working carefully, Morris gets two strikes on Smith. Then, with the count at 1 and 2, he pours in a high, hard one on the outer edge of the plate. Goodbye baseball. Dixie, here we come.

Joe Carter says it all, leaning his head against the right-field wall after watching the ball sail into the Braves bullpen.

David Wells, Mike Timlin and Mark Eichhorn hold the Braves at bay for the next four innings, to keep the pen's record perfect in the Series. But Jays hitters, who had looked like they were starting to solve fireballer John Smoltz earlier, were shut down the rest of the way by Smoltz and the Braves' ace reliever, Mike Stanton. Their fine perfor-mances cut the Jays' Series lead to one, three games to two.

Some Braves hitters claimed to have been given a little extra incentive at the plate by the announcement, before Game 5 was even under way, of plans for a Blue Jay victory parade. The also didn't like Alomar and Gruber mimicking the Atlanta tomahawk chop.

The only Jay to rock Smoltz was hot-hitting Pat Borders, whose .438 average after Game 5 was double his teammates' total. Borders drove in both runs and blocked two Morris pitches in the dirt at crucial moments. But Atlanta continued to run wild against him and any starter whose name wasn't Jimmy Key.

The theft total had hit 13, and the sheriff's department back in Atlanta wasn't likely to do a darn thing about it.

RICK EGLINTON

RIGHT: SAY IT ISN'T SO, JOE. CARTER LEANS HEAD AGAINST RIGHT-FIELD WALL AFTER WATCHING GRAND SLAM SAIL OVER.

BELOW: BLOWOUT HAD ACTRESS JANE FONDA GIVING HIGH FIVES INSTEAD OF PRAYING.

RICHARD LAUTENS

THE TASTE OF VICTORY . . . AT LAST

GAME 6

Jays 4 at Braves 3

So, at long last, this is how it tastes.

Sweet, bubbly and intoxicating.

The incredible taste of *victory* — for a team, a city and a nation.

A refreshing taste to ease our pain, soothe our souls and warm our hearts. Forever.

Come, let us sip from the cup of memories, overflowing with delicious moments from Dave Winfield, Pat Borders, Jimmy Key and others who concocted the most thrilling game in Toronto's sports history . . .

So, where were *you* at two minutes to midnight on Saturday, Oct. 24, 1992? Were you one of the 45,551 Jay lovers living and dying with every pitch beamed from Atlanta-Fulton County Stadium to the JumboTron at the SkyDome? Or were you among the millions watching, listening (and praying) in homes, pubs and workplaces across the nation?

It's 11:58 p.m. and Canada's first World Series championship is just one strike away. But nobody is taking anything for granted — especially Tom Henke and Otis Nixon.

Fourteen minutes earlier, when Henke had taken the mound with a 2-1 lead, we were cautiously optimistic. The Blue Jays bullpen hadn't surrendered a run in 15⅓ innings, nor blown a save chance since July 24. Henke had yet to give up so much as a hit to the Braves.

But when leadoff hitter Jeff Blauser slashes a single to left on Henke's third pitch, stomachs begin to tighten. Damon Berryhill sacrifices Blauser to second, and the tying run is just a base hit away.

Enter Lonnie Smith, destroyer of the Jays' hopes with a grand slam in Game 5. Henke gets two quick strikes, but Smith fouls off three tough pitches and walks on a 3-and-2 count.

Now, on this night when we turn our clocks back to Standard time, Francisco Cabrera digs in at the plate — hoping to clean our clocks and set them back 10 days.

Yes, the hero of Atlanta's miraculous, last-gasp victory over Pittsburgh in the NL playoffs would love to do it again. *Craaack!*

There's a line drive to left. Omigod! Candy Maldonado has misjudged the ball, starting in. Now he LEAPS and . . . juuuust snares it in the webbing of his glove.

Whew! Two out, but Nixon is up and you *know* he's dangerous. As the Tomahawk Chop wails, Nixon quickly falls behind 0 and 2 to Henke. One more strike and the Blue Jays are world cham. . .

WINNING WHOOP FROM KELLY GRUBER AS MIKE TIMLIN
FIELDS BUNT AND TOSSES TO JOE CARTER FOR FINAL OUT.

COLIN McCONNELL

91

Craaack! Base hit to left! Blauser is rounding third. Maldonado's throw is awaaay high. Tie game.

BONG! At the stroke of midnight, it seems the Jays' golden carriage to baseball immortality has turned into a pumpkin.

But hold on. Ron Gant flies out to Devon White to ensure extra innings, and there's more to come — much more.

Mind you, there are many who feel this game really shouldn't be close. Hadn't the Jays rapped at least one base hit in every inning, chasing Braves starter Steve Avery after four?

Check the boxscore and you'll find the answer under LOB. Through nine innings, the Jays have stranded 11 runners. Winfield, the cleanup man, is the most obvious underachiever: 0 for 4 through nine, with only one RBI in 21 at-bats in the Series.

Jays starter David Cone has pitched well but received minimal run support, as usual: a Maldonado solo homer in the fourth, and a first-inning score by White when Dave Justice erred on Joe Carter's liner to right-centre.

When he leaves after six innings and 103 pitches, Cone has given up only one run, on a Terry Pendleton sacrifice fly, and stands to win what might be his last game as a Blue Jay.

In the seventh, after Nixon lashes a two-out single off Todd Stottlemyre, two wonderful things happen for the Jays:

1. When Cito Gaston elects to replace Stottlemyre with lefthander David Wells, Bobby Cox counters by replacing lefthanded-hitting Deion Sanders with righthanded-hitting Gant. Jay-killer Sanders, with eight hits in the Series, including two hits and two stolen bases tonight, is replaced by a guy hitting .167.

2. Wells proceeds to do what no Jays pitcher but Key has been able to manage: keep the baserunner close to first with a good pickoff move. As a result, Borders, who has allowed an embarrassing 15 steals in this Series (and 16 in the Oakland playoffs), is given a fighting chance and throws out Nixon to end the inning.

After that play, there is no doubt that Borders, going 9 for 20 as the only player in the Series to hit in all six games (and extending his post-season hitting streak to a record 14 games, including the last two against Minnesota in '91), would be named World Series MVP.

So, where were we? Oh, yes, extra innings.

As Saturday night becomes Sunday morning, many who have been at the SkyDome for more than six hours are on their feet, waving flags and brandishing foam-rubber Js.

At home, millions of us are asking: How long can this go on? Will we be going through this again tomorrow night?

As the 10th unfolds, chances of a quick kill seem remote.

JEFF GOODE

SERIES MVP PAT BORDERS IS A DEAD DUCK AT THE PLATE AS BRAVES CATCHER DAMON BERRYHILL TAKES A THROW FROM DEION SANDERS AND BLOCKS THE PLATE. BUT PAT IS A TEDDY BEAR AFTER THE GAME AS HE GETS VICTORY KISS FROM DAUGHTER LINDSAY RAE.

COLIN McCONNELL

92

RIGHT: NICE GAME, SAYS JOE CARTER AS HE WALKS PITCHER DAVID CONE BACK TO THE DUGOUT. CONE LEFT THE GAME AFTER SIX INNINGS WITH A 2-1 LEAD.

COLIN McCONNELL

ABOVE: DAVE WINFIELD GETS CONGRATULATIONS FROM TEAMMATES IN THE DUGOUT AFTER HIS 11TH-INNING TWO-RUN DOUBLE THAT SCORED THE WINNING RUN.

COLIN McCONNELL

All keyed up!

BLUE JAYS 4 at BRAVES 3
Game Six

Toronto	ab	r	h	bi	bb	so	avg.
White cf	5	2	2	0	0	1	.231
RAlomar 2b	6	1	3	0	0	0	.208
Carter 1b	5	0	2	1	0	0	.273
Winfield rf	5	0	1	2	1	0	.227
Maldonado lf	6	1	2	1	0	0	.158
Gruber 3b	4	0	1	0	0	0	.105
Borders c	4	0	2	0	1	0	.450
Lee ss	4	0	1	0	0	1	.105
Tabler ph	1	0	0	0	0	0	.000
Griffin ss	0	0	0	0	0	0	—
Cone p	2	0	0	0	1	0	.500
Stottlemyre p	0	0	0	0	0	0	—
Wells p	0	0	0	0	0	0	—
c-DBell ph	1	0	0	0	0	0	.000
DWard p	0	0	0	0	0	0	—
Henke p	0	0	0	0	0	0	—
Key p	1	0	0	0	0	0	.000
Timlin p	0	0	0	0	0	0	—
Totals	44	4	14	4	3	2	
Atlanta	ab	r	h	bi	bb	so	avg.
Nixon cf	6	0	2	1	0	0	.296
DSanders lf	3	1	2	0	0	0	.533
Gant ph-lf	2	0	0	0	0	0	.125
Pendleton 3b	4	0	1	1	0	2	.240
Justice rf	4	0	0	0	1	1	.158
Bream 1b	3	0	0	0	2	0	.200
Blauser ss	5	2	3	0	0	1	.250
Berryhill c	4	0	0	0	0	1	.091
1-Smoltz pr	0	0	0	0	0	0	.000
Lemke 2b	2	0	0	1	1	1	.211
LSmith ph	0	0	0	0	1	0	.167
Belliard 2b	0	0	0	0	0	0	—
Avery p	1	0	0	0	0	1	.000
PSmith p	1	0	0	0	0	0	.000
Treadway ph	1	0	0	0	0	0	.000
Stanton p	0	0	0	0	0	0	—
Wohlers p	0	0	0	0	0	0	—
Cabrera ph	1	0	0	0	0	0	.000
Leibrandt p	0	0	0	0	0	0	—
g-Hunter ph	1	0	0	1	0	0	.200

E—Griffin (1), Justice (1). LOB—Toronto 13, Atlanta 10. 2B—Carter 2 (2), Winfield (1), Borders (3), DSanders (2). HR—Maldonado (1) off Avery. RBIs—Carter (3), Winfield 2 (3), Maldonado (2), Nixon (1), Pendleton (2), Hunter (2). SB—White (1), RAlomar (3), DSanders 2 (5). CS—Nixon (1). S—Gruber, Berryhill, Belliard. SF—Carter, Pendleton. GIDP—Cone.

Toronto	ip	h	r	er	bb	so	np	era
Cone	6	4	1	1	3	6	103	3.48
Stottlemyre	2/3	1	0	0	0	1	11	0.00
Wells	1/3	0	0	0	0	0	4	0.00
DWard	1	0	0	0	1	1	16	0.00
Henke	1 1/3	2	1	1	1	0	33	2.70
Key W, 2-0	1 1/3	1	1	0	0	0	14	1.00
Timlin S, 1	1/3	0	0	0	0	0	2	0.00
Atlanta	ip	h	r	er	bb	so	np	era
Avery	4	6	2	2	2	2	60	3.75
PSmith	3	3	0	0	0	0	39	0.00
Stanton	1 2/3	2	0	0	1	0	15	0.00
Wohlers	1/3	0	0	0	0	0	5	0.00
Leibrandt L, 0-1	2	3	2	2	0	0	35	9.00

How the runs scored

Jays' first: White led off with a single to left. White stole second. Alomar grounded out, second to first, advancing White to third. Carter drove in White. **Blue Jays 1, Braves 0.**

Braves' third: Sanders doubled off first baseman Carter's glove. Sanders stole third. Pendleton's sacrifice fly to centre drove in Sanders. **Blue Jays 1, Braves 1.**

Jays' fourth: Maldonado hit a 1-0 pitch to left-centre for his first homer. **Blue Jays 2, Braves 1.**

Braves ninth: Blauser led off with a single to left. Berryhill's sacrifice bunt, advanced him to second. Pinch-hitter Smith drew a walk. Pinch-hitter Cabrera lined out to left. Nixon singled to left, scoring Blauser. **Blue Jays 2, Braves 2.**

Jays' 11th: Key fouled out to first. White walked. Alomar singled to centre; White to second. Carter flew out to centre. Winfield doubled down the line in left, driving in White and Alomar. **Blue Jays 4, Braves 2.**

Braves' 11th: Blauser singled. Berryhill safe on Griffin's fielding error at short; Blauser to third. Belliard's sacrifice bunt, pitcher to second covering at first, advanced Smoltz to second. Pinch-hitter Hunter grounded out, driving in Blauser. **Blue Jays 4, Braves 3.**

Lefthander Charlie Leibrandt, winning pitcher in the Jays' heartbreaking Game 7 loss to Kansas City in the '85 playoffs, handles them easily. And Key, picking up for Henke with one out in the 10th, has no trouble with Justice and Sid Bream.

Key, however, does have problems in the 11th — because Cito *sends him up to bat.*

With his bullpen reduced to Mike Timlin and Mark Eichhorn, Cito wants to keep the steady lefty in there. In the first at-bat of his nine-year major league career, Key works Leibrandt to a 2-and-2 count, then pops up to Bream.

When White is hit by a pitch and Roberto Alomar follows by lining a changeup to centre field, the Jays have another splendid scoring chance.

Can they finally cash in? Not with Carter. He lifts a routine fly to centre and it's two out with Winfield up.

So far, Big Dave's main contribution to this game has been with his glove — a tumbling, turf-tearing, backhanded catch of a sinking Gant liner in the eighth that saved a triple.

Now, on a 3-and-2 count, Winfield *swings* and rips a double between third baseman Pendleton and the bag.

Here comes White! In left, Gant is still chasing the ball! White is waving Alomar home. Horns are blaring on Yonge St. It's 4-2 Jays.

This time, it's got to be over. Uh-uh-uhhh! You know better than that. You know this team never makes it easy.

Five minutes later, there is no cheering in Toronto.

A Blauser first-pitch single followed by a shocking bad-bounce error by Alfredo Griffin on a perfect double play ball has put runners on the corners. A sacrifice bunt by Rafael Belliard and the tying run is at second, one out.

As that infernal Tomahawk Chop swells and reverberates, pinch-hitter Brian Hunter's grounder to first baseman Carter scores Atlanta's third run. The tying run, pinch-runner John Smoltz, is on third.

And look who's coming up: Nixon, the nemesis from the ninth. But he won't face Key. Cito, mindful that Nixon has hit .343 against lefthanders versus .263 against righthanders, waves to the bullpen for Timlin.

Mike Timlin! Is he kidding? A relative greenhorn — who had jumped from Double A ball to the majors last year, had arm problems and was trying to get it together in Class A as recently as July — charged with getting the most pressure-packed out in Blue Jays history?

Hey, Cito's running this team and he knows best. Haven't you learned that by now?

Nixon fouls one off. Then, he bunts! Timlin bounces off the mound, scoops it and calmly throws to Carter at first. IT'S OVER!

Now we can taste it. *Victory.* Horns can blare. People can yell. A city can go nuts, and a nation can smile from coast to coast.

At last, our Blue Jays are champs.
WORLD CHAMPS, EH?

COLIN McCONNELL

WINNING PITCHER JIMMY KEY CELEBRATES WITH ED SPRAGUE'S WIFE, KRISTEN, AFTER SURVIVING THE VICTORY PILE-UP WHICH CATCHER PAT BORDERS LEAPS ABOARD (BELOW).

DALE BRAZAO

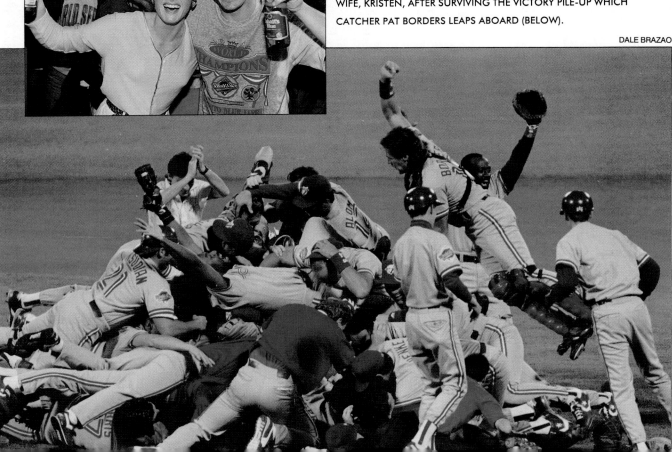

RICK MADONIK

FRANTIC FANS AT
SKYDOME CHEERED ON
THE JAYS FROM AFAR.
MORE THAN 45,000
SHOWED UP TO WATCH
THE GAME ON THE
JUMBOTRON.

WALL-TO-WALL PEOPLE
JAMMED YONGE ST.
AFTER THE GAME TO
CELEBRATE CANADA'S
FIRST WORLD SERIES
VICTORY.

KEN FAUGHT

INDIVIDUAL ACHIEVEMENTS

Batting

Between them, Joe Carter and Roberto Alomar finished in the top 10 in 11 key offensive categories during the '92 AL season:

Batting average .... Alomar .310
Seventh behind Edgar Martinez, .343

Runs .... Alomar 105
Third behind Tony Phillips, 114

Home runs: .... Carter 34
Tied for fourth behind Juan Gonzalez, 43

RBIs .... Carter 119
Second behind Cecil Fielder, 124

Stolen bases .... Alomar 49
Fifth behind Kenny Lofton, 66

On base percentage .... Alomar .405
Third behind Frank Thomas, .439

Total bases .... Carter 310
Second behind Kirby Puckett, 313

Hits .... Alomar 177
Tenth behind Kirby Puckett, 210

Slugging percentage .... Carter .498
Sixth behind Mark McGwire, .585

Extra base hits .... Carter 71
Second behind Frank Thomas, 72

Triples .... Alomar 8
Tied for fifth behind Lance Johnson, 12

Dave Winfield was in the top 10 in RBIs (108), total bases (286), slugging percentage (.491) and extra-base hits (92).

Pitching

Several Jays pitchers were in the top 10 in key pitching categories:

Wins .... Jack Morris 21
Tied for first with Kevin Brown

Earned run average .... Juan Guzman 2.64
Fourth in AL behind Roger Clemens, 2.41

Saves .... Tom Henke 34
Fifth behind Dennis Eckersley, 51

Game appearances Duane Ward 79
Second behind Kenny Rogers, 81

Strikeouts .... Guzman 165
Ninth behind Randy Johnson, 241

Opponents' batting average .... Guzman .207
Second behind Randy Johnson, .206

Winning percentage .... Morris .778
Second behind Mike Mussina, .783

Innings pitched .... Morris 240.2
Tenth behind Kevin Brown, 265.2

Guzman was third in winning percentage and second in strikeouts per nine innings. Juan was also second in wild pitches, with 14, and Jimmy Key was ninth in home runs allowed, with 24.

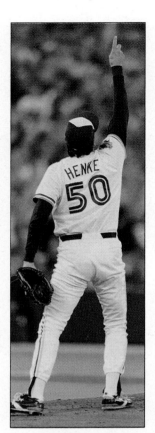

WORLD SERIES MOMENTS: FROM TOP, TOM HENKE PAT BORDERS AND KELLY GRUBER.

FINAL STANDINGS

American League / National League

EAST

	W	L	Pct	Gb	Last 10		W	L	Pct	Gb	Last 10
Toronto	96	66	.593	—	7-3	Pittsburgh	96	66	.593	—	7-3
Milwaukee	92	70	.568	4	7-3	Montreal	87	75	.537	9	4-6
Baltimore	89	73	.549	7	6-4	St. Louis	83	79	.512	13	6-4
Cleveland	76	86	.469	20	4-6	Chicago	78	84	.481	18	3-7
New York	76	86	.469	20	4-6	New York	72	90	.444	24	3-7
Detroit	75	87	.463	21	4-6	Philadelphia	70	92	.432	26	6-4
Boston	73	89	.451	23	6-4						

WEST

	W	L	Pct	Gb	Last 10		W	L	Pct	Gb	Last 10
Oakland	96	66	.593	—	4-6	Atlanta	98	64	.605	—	7-3
Minnesota	90	72	.556	6	6-4	Cincinnati	90	72	.556	8	5-5
Chicago	86	76	.531	10	4-6	San Diego	82	80	.506	16	3-7
Texas	77	85	.475	19	5-5	Houston	81	81	.500	17	8-2
California	72	90	.444	24	5-5	San Fran.	72	90	.444	26	5-5
Kansas City	72	90	.444	24	4-6	L. Angeles	63	99	.389	35	2-8
Seattle	64	98	.395	32	6-4						

Jays' Batting

	AVG	G	AB	R	H	TB	2B	3B	HR	RBI	BB	SO	SB	E
Alomar	.310	152	571	105	177	244	27	8	8	76	87	52	49	5
Bell	.242	61	161	23	39	57	6	3	2	15	15	34	7	0
Borders	.242	138	480	47	116	185	26	2	13	53	33	75	1	8
Carter	.264	158	622	97	164	310	30	7	34	119	36	109	12	9
Ducey	.048	23	21	3	1	2	1	0	0	0	0	10	0	0
Griffin	.233	63	150	21	35	42	7	0	0	10	9	19	3	7
Gruber	.229	120	446	42	102	157	16	3	11	43	26	72	7	17
Kent	.240	65	192	36	46	85	13	1	8	35	20	47	2	11
Knorr	.263	8	19	1	5	8	0	0	1	2	1	5	0	0
Lee	.263	128	396	49	104	125	10	1	3	39	50	73	6	7
Maksudian	.000	3	3	0	0	0	0	0	0	0	0	0	0	0
Maldonado	.272	137	489	64	133	226	25	4	20	66	59	12	2	6
Martinez	.625	7	8	2	5	8	0	0	1	3	0	1	0	0
Mulliniks	.500	3	2	1	1	1	0	0	0	0	1	0	0	0
Myers	.230	22	61	4	14	23	6	0	1	13	5	5	0	1
Olerud	.284	138	458	68	130	206	28	0	16	66	70	61	1	7
Quinlan	.067	13	15	2	1	2	1	0	0	2	2	9	0	1
Sprague	.234	22	47	6	11	16	2	0	1	7	3	7	0	1
Tabler	.252	49	135	11	34	39	5	0	0	16	11	14	0	0
Ward	.345	18	29	7	10	16	3	0	1	3	4	4	0	0
White	.248	153	641	98	159	250	26	7	17	60	47	133	37	7
Winfield	.290	156	583	92	169	286	33	3	26	108	82	89	2	0
Zosky	.286	8	7	1	2	4	0	1	0	1	0	2	0	1
Pitchers	.000	162	0	0	0	0	0	0	0	0	0	0	0	5
Totals	**.263**	**162**	**5536**	**780**	**1458**	**2292**	**265**	**40**	**163**	**737**	**561**	**933**	**129**	**93**

Jays' Pitching

	W	L	ERA	G	GS	CG	SV	IP	H	R	ER	HR	BB	SO
Cone	4	3	2.55	8	7	0	0	53.0	39	16	15	3	29	47
Eichhorn	2	0	4.35	23	0	0	0	31.0	35	15	15	1	7	19
Guzman	1	5	2.64	28	28	1	0	180.2	135	56	53	6	72	165
Henke	6	2	2.26	57	0	0	34	55.2	40	19	14	5	22	46
Hentgen	5	2	5.36	28	2	0	0	50.1	49	30	30	7	32	39
Key	13	13	3.53	33	33	4	0	216.2	205	88	85	24	59	117
Leiter	0	0	9.00	1	0	0	0	1.0	1	1	1	0	2	0
Linton	1	3	8.63	8	3	0	0	24.0	31	23	23	5	17	16
MacDonald	1	0	4.37	27	0	0	0	47.1	50	24	23	4	16	26
Morris	21	6	4.04	34	34	6	0	240.2	222	114	108	18	80	132
Stieb	4	6	5.04	21	14	1	0	96.1	98	58	54	9	43	45
Stottlemyre	12	11	4.50	28	27	6	0	174.0	175	99	87	20	63	98
Tomlin	0	2	4.12	26	0	0	1	43.2	45	23	20	0	20	35
Talicek	0	0	10.80	2	0	0	0	1.2	2	2	2	0	2	1
Ward	7	4	1.95	79	0	0	12	101.1	76	27	22	5	39	103
Weathers	0	0	8.10	2	0	0	0	3.1	5	3	3	1	2	3
Wells	7	9	5.40	41	14	0	2	120.0	138	84	72	16	36	62
Totals	**96**	**66**	**3.91**	**162**	**162**	**18**	**49**	**1440.2**	**1346**	**682**	**626**	**124**	**541**	**954**

Jays' season records

Batting	.263	Tied for fourth behind Twins,	.277
Runs	780	Second behind Detroit,	791
Homers	163	Tied for second behind Detroit,	182
Pitching (ERA)	3.91	Ninth behind Brewers,	3.43
Pitching (wins)	96	Tied for first with Oakland	
Fielding average	.985	Fourth behind Milwaukee,	.986
Strikeouts	954	Second behind Texas,	1034
Walks	541	Seventh behind Milwaukee,	435
Attendance	4,028,318	First ahead of Baltimore,	3,567,819